PYTRE, SON OF DOG

Happy Birthday LISA

James S. Earl

5 MARCH 2018

PYTRE, SON OF DOG

James S. Earl

Rev. date: 02/12/2016

To order additional copies of this book, contact:
Xlibris
1-888-795-4274
www.Xlibris.com
Orders@Xlibris.com
540412

CONTENTS

Chapter One: Happy Birthday 1

Chapter Two: Puppy Love 5

Chapter Three: Wounded in Action 9

Chapter Four: Snakes 13

Chapter Five: Trauma Hospital 17

Chapter Six: Chasing Birds 21

Chapter Seven: The Meeting 24

Chapter Eight: The Sermon on the Bank 28

Chapter Nine: The Meeting Number Two 32

Chapter Ten: Crucifixion 37

Chapter Eleven: The Meeting Number Three 43

Chapter Twelve: Carnival Freaks 50

Chapter Thirteen: Meeting of the Witnesses.................................54

Chapter Fourteen: 9th Floor, Norfolk General Hospital 65

Chapter Fifteen: Big Meeting Number One 69

Chapter Sixteen: Dog Pound...72

Chapter Seventeen: Impromptu Meeting.......................................78

Chapter Eighteen: Dog Gone It 83

Chapter Nineteen: Confusion and Promotion................................86

Chapter Twenty: Smithy 89

Chapter Twenty-One: Hey, Samson's Friend 93

Chapter Twenty Two: Ma and Company 99

Chapter Twenty Three: Executive Order 622014 105

Chapter Twenty Four: The Hit..108

Chapter Twenty Five: Down the Rabbit Hole....................................111

Chapter Twenty Six: Christmas Party..115

Chapter Twenty Seven: Fred 118

THE PROFESSOR SERIES

The Professor: The Anti-Semitic and The Jew 121

The Professor Two: Sergeant Jimbo and the Band of Love Children....126

The Professor Three: Smoking and the Single Mom 135

Homecoming 145

In Loving Memory of all our Canine Friends
Who are no longer with us.

In Grateful Honor of Current and Future Fur Buddies.

Special Thanks to Rocky J. Earl, pictured on author's
photo, no matter what was going on in the house, when I
started writing, he would come in, crawl under my desk,
and sleep with his head on my feet. I love you boy.

CHAPTER ONE

Happy Birthday

Ranchita, California
2 JUNE 2011

Curt opened the gate to his favorite outdoor café, a dog friendly place called *Rock Hounds*. His faithful companion Samson trotted through the gate, sat down, and obediently waited for Curt to enter. Curt shut the gate, and headed for his favorite table. It was in the back, up against a storage shed. A habit they had both picked up from the military. No one could sneak up on him. As he passed the dog, Samson, a mostly German Shepard and Belgian Malinois mix, fell into step at his right rear. They both were convalescing from injuries they had received in Afghanistan many months earlier.

Both the man and the dog intently, but non-intrusively, scanned the crowd. A group of drunken workers, their shift having ended a while ago, were loudly carrying on. Curt caught some words like 'bin Laden.' Normally this would have put him on high alert, but the President had announced the killing of Osama bin Laden a month ago. In this mostly liberal section of the San Diego area, bin Laden was a common topic. Then there was Karen, the waitress, and Sam, the owner and bartender. No apparent threats here. Curt relaxed a little and took his usual seat. Samson lay down under the table, facing outward.

"The usual Curt," Karen asked, "A small pitcher of beer, a bowl of ice water, plus two plates of ribs, and a side of fried pickles?"

Curt smiled. *Rock Hounds* had the best BBQ ribs and best fried pickles in the world. Not to mention that Karen was a very attractive woman. That's probably why he only came here when it was her shift.

"Well, it's not that hot today," Curt said. "So let's change that bowl of water into a bowl of cold milk."

Karen got down on the floor and scratched Samson's head. "You are such a good boy," she said. "You both take care of each other above all else." Karen got up. "Thank you, Curt," she said, and swished away.

"You're welcome Karen," Curt said to her back as he watched her walk away. His gaze followed her toward the bar.

As his survey roamed, Curt sat up with a start. He was instantly alert. There was someone else in the café. One of the oddest looking people Curt had every seen. The man was in a mirror position from Curt, his back to the wall against the rest rooms. He was facing out toward the crowd. How had Curt missed him? This man was the epitome of stealth. Samson, alerting to his master's discomfort, stiffened, and looked over at the man. Then Samson let out a little whine, and began wagging his tail.

"What the hell is wrong with you Samson?" Curt asked. "You have been convalescing too long." Samson let out another little whine, but continued to intermittently wag his tail.

When the food arrived, Karen put one plate of ribs and the bowl of milk on the floor in front of Samson. When she stood up Curt whispered to her, "Who is the stranger in the corner?"

"Don't know," Karen whispered back. "He got here about thirty minutes ago. Neither Sam nor I have every seen him before, and we would remember something like that if we had. He has a strange appetite too. After his fourth glass of milk, Sam had me bring him a large pitcher. Also, he got the ribs. I know, they are our specialty, but he has been gnawing on the bones. There are still uneaten ribs on the plate!"

Both Curt and Karen looked over at the stranger. The man looked up, and smiled. Karen looked away, but Curt held his gaze. A peace fell over Curt. This man seemed so very gentle, with such a beautiful smile, but what a hard looking man from what you could see. He wore long sleeves. In fact the only part of his body that was exposed was his head, neck, and hands. His ethnicity would be impossible to place. His skin color was a mixture of black, brown, white, and yellow. Not a blend, but patchy. In fact, the patch from his nose to as far down the neck as you could see was spotted, or maybe layered in brown and black. It was brindle. This didn't seem to be due to injury, like from a fire. However, the man had injuries. Around his neck was a deep circular gash that looked like he had been hung, or garroted. There was a diagonal scar across his left, white check that crossed over his nose and ended on his yellow forehead. The bottom of his right ear was missing. The man raised the rib he was eating and motioned Curt over. This time Curt looked away. Samson mewed, and wagged his tail.

Curt ate his food while silently mulling over this new enigma. Occasionally he would glance over at the man, but the man was intently concentrating on his food. Samson dug into his ribs, and lapped up his milk.

Curt was startled by a loud commotion. The group of drunks were getting up and heading toward him. Samson went on crouched alert, but remained silent, unmoving.

"Excuse me, kind sir," said the lead drunk. "If you could help me, and my distinguished colleagues with a bit of a dispute. Who is the greatest Seal team in the world?"

Curt was disoriented for a brief second, poised on a surrealistic world. Then understanding dawned. Fucking bin Laden, he thought. Then he became angry. Curt, Lieutenant Curtis Mays, United States Navy, would like nothing better that to leap up, and grab this young punk by the throat and yell, "Seal Team 3, Trident K9 Warriors, for which I am the deputy commander!" However, that would be unprofessional, and he was a professional. You know loose lips, and all that good stuff. In a second he had regained his composure.

"What was the Team that got bin Laden?" Curt asked.

The crowd of drunks began whooping. Some started chanting, "Seal Team Six!" They moved off. Someone deposited a full beer at Curt's table. They moved toward the stranger in the corner.

"How many Seal Teams are there?" One drunk asked.

"Must be hundreds of them," another man said.

"Naw, there is probably only about ten," piped in another guy.

As they approached the strangers table they slowed. Curt smiled. The man in the corner did have a sobering effect on people. The lead drunk approached, and gave a bow. Before he could speak, the stranger looked up from his food, and said, "Seal Team Three is my favorite."

The crowd murmured in confusion. Curt was instantly on high alert. "Why Team Three?" A man from the crowd asked.

"I know one of the team members," the stranger replied.

"You know a seal?" asked the leader.

The stranger laughed. "I think you are thinking of the circus. There are no actual seals on the seal teams."

"I know that smartass," said the lead drunk. "I mean you know someone that is a Navy Seal?"

"No,' said the stranger. "I don't know any of the people that are Navy Seals, but I know Samson. I'm going to meet him here. Today is his birthday."

"Whatever," said the lead drunk. Confused and tiring of the game, the crowd shuffled off to the TV room. The lead drunk signaled Karen for another round for the group. Curt's head was reeling. Maybe he had PTSD or something. How did that man know Samson's name. He was sure neither he nor Karen had mentioned it. And how the hell could he know it was Samson's birthday. Probably only two people in the world knew that. He had to find out who this man was. As Curt stood up, the stranger nodded him over. Samson took off like a shot.

"Samson, no!" Curt yelled. But Samson was already there, standing on his hind legs, licking the stranger on his face. As Curt rushed up, Samson rolled on his back, and the stranger reached down, and started scratching Samson's belly. A twinge of jealousy tugged at Curt.

As Curt watched, the stranger got on his knees, and while one hand scratched Samson's belly, the other hand gently rubbed the thirteen inch scar that extended from the chunk taken out of Samson's right shoulder through his right flank.

"AK-47 assault rifle?" The stranger asked. Samson nodded yes.

"Yes," said Curt, and then realized that Samson had nodded. "Just who the hell are you?'

The man slowly stood up, extended his hand, and said' "Pytre."

"How do you know me?" Curt asked.

"I don't know you," Pytre said. "But if you are a friend of Samson, you are a friend of mine. Happy birthday boy." Samson began wagging his tail in earnest.

"Okay," Curt said. "Samson saved my life in Afghanistan, and if you…"

But Pytre interrupted him, "Braafy Samson!"

Curt stopped, "You know how to speak Dutch?"

"Not really," said Pytre. "I don't really know how to speak English. We're just communicating here."

"You stay right here," Curt said shaking his finger at the man's face. Damn, he thought. He had left his cell phone at home. He had to tell Headquarters about this guy. He raced to the bar to use the phone. Sam was coming in from the TV room. As he turned he saw that Pytre was gone. Not a trace. Samson came sauntering up to him, wagging his tail. Curt sat down hard. This was crazy.

Karen was now at the stranger's table. "Hey," she said. She was smiling. "Our strange friend bought your meal, and left a very good tip." She held up a hundred dollar bill and a napkin. Reading the napkin, Karen said, "Happy birthday Samson. It was so nice to meet your friend. This should cover all our meals."

CHAPTER TWO

Puppy Love

Bethlehem, Judea
25 December, 33 BC

Mary cuddled the Baby Jesus. It had been a very difficult year. Both for her and Joseph, but it had all been worth it. She had never felt such peace and contentment as she did at that very moment. Jesus was such a special baby. She guessed all moms felt that way, but Jesus was going to grow up to be a very special man. She had that on the highest authority. Her thoughts were interrupted as Joseph hurriedly entered the stable.

"Mary," he said. "We have a guest. Actually, we have three of them. They are wise men from the East. They have come to see Jesus." Joseph was smiling.

Mary jostled Jesus into an upright position. "Well," she said. "Please show them in." Joseph pulled open the curtain, and the three magi entered the stable. They immediately dropped to their knees in front of Jesus, and bowed their heads.

"Please," Mary said. "Welcome Jesus. Today is his first day after being born." The three magi raised their heads. Their eyes were full of joyous tears. They walked on their knees the few feet to the baby, and began making cooing sounds. Jesus smiled.

After several minutes of this, the tallest magi stood up, and said, "My name is Malika, I come from Persia. My two companions come from Babylon. A great star hangs in the sky over this very stable. It led us here from afar. It has prophesized the birth of a new savior; this baby that you have told us is called Jesus. We have brought gifts for Jesus. Will you allow me to go get them?" Mary nodded.

Malika exited the stable, and headed to the inn where their caravan awaited. He approached his camel, and grabbed the rear saddle box. This contained the wonderful gifts. There was a leather pouch full of gold coins and trinkets. There was a silk cloth wrapped around a bundle of concentrated frankincense, and there was a glass bottle of liquid myrrh. Malika reflected with pride that these were very nice gifts for the new king.

As Malika turned to leave, a yapping sound could be heard from his side saddle box, and a mixed breed, multicolored puppy popped his head out of the box.

Malika grinned, and said "Pytre, my friend." He reached over and scratched the puppy's ears. "I have not forgotten you, or my promise."

Malika reflected on that last day, as he was preparing to debark from Persia to follow the star. His youngest boy had come running up to him with tears in his eyes. He was carrying the limp body of Pytre.

"What is it Cy?" Malika asked. Now Cy was openly weeping.

"Father," he said. "A snake has killed my dog and all her pups. Only the runt Pytre is still alive, and he is in very bad shape." Malika ached for his son, and took the limp puppy from Cy. The dog was barely breathing, and had been bitten on his right ear. In fact, the snake had torn the bottom of his right ear off. That may have been what saved his life. It probably tore the poison out of the body with the ear part.

Cy was sobbing uncontrollably now. In between sobs he said, "Father, can you take Pytre to see the new king? Maybe he can save him."

Malika's chest hurt from the sadness. Holding Pytre in one hand, and hugging his son close to him with the other, he said, "Cy, I promise you. I will take Pytre on the trip, and if he survives, I will introduce him to the new king."

Cy visibly relaxed, and hugged his father even tighter. "Thank you father," he said.

That was three months ago Malika reflected. Pytre had made a remarkable recovery on the trip. Malika had fallen in love with him.

"Not now my friend," Malika said, continuing to scratch Pytre's head. "Let me give the gifts, and then you can meet the baby king." Malika turned and walked toward the stable.

However, Pytre had other ideas. When Malika entered the stable, Pytre leaped from the box on the camel's back, and limped off toward the stables.

"Behold," said Malika. "We bring you gifts." Malika pulled the gifts from the box, and placed them in front of Mary and Jesus. Joseph was ecstatic. Mary was extremely pleased. Jesus had fallen back asleep.

The curtain to the stall slightly parted, and Pytre entered. He went up to the baby, and licked his foot. Jesus smiled and woke up. Pytre leaped in Mary's lap and started licking Jesus' face. Jesus started giggling.

"He's adorable," Mary squealed, and started scratching the side of Pytre's head. Joseph kneeled down beside the wise men, and started rubbing on the puppy. The one day old Baby Jesus reached up with his right hand and grabbed the fur on the side of Pytre's head. Pytre closed his eyes, laid his head on Jesus' chest, and began to purr.

"Damn," muttered Malika. There were tears in his eyes. He got up and walked out of the stall. "I really wanted to take that dog home." The other two magi, in alarm, followed him out.

"Malika," they said in unison. "This is like the word of God."

"I hear what the Lord is saying damn it," snapped Malika. He grabbed both men by an ear and squeezed hard. "I just don't have to be happy about it now." Then he softened. Babylonians just didn't have the same passion that Persians did. "Relax," he said. "Of course I'm going to do it. After all, I am a wise man."

The three magi reentered the stall. Joseph, Mary, Jesus, and Pytre were all laughing, and having a real good time. The wise men joined in. It was a wondrous moment.

As the moment passed, Malika said, "His name is Pytre. He is the son of Peeps, the runt, and only survivor of a vicious serpent attack."

At this, Mary and Joseph exchanged knowing glances. "Fitting," Joseph said.

"Pytre's father is unknown," Malika continued. "As it is our perceived notion of these things with dogs. Although I suspect it is a Shepard dog from the Rocks. And now he is Jesus' puppy. The most coveted position in the canine world."

Mary shook her head, and said, "You are quite the showman aren't you?"

Malika stood at full attention, and bowed his head. "Yes ma'am," he said. "Please take good care of him."

"The Lord has trusted me with his son," she said. "Trust that Pytre will be taken care of too. God's will be done."

"God's will be done." The magi echoed, and left the stable.

The three magi approached the caravan, and mounted their camels. As they were settling in their mounts, Malika said, "King Herod wanted us to make a return visit to him on our way out of here." The other two magi wheeled on him.

"Are you insane," one of them said. "He murdered his own son. While we were there we witnessed him stomping a dog to death while in a rage."

"He is very unstable," the other one said. "It is best not to return."

Malika grinned ear to ear. "Passion from Babylonians," he said. "Today is truly a glorious day. Besides, I hear Damascus is great this time of year."

They all laughed, and headed their caravan north.

"Besides," Malika continued. "King Herod is a donkey's ass." The whole caravan was laughing now. A few miles out of town, Malika slowed, and turned back to look at Bethlehem.

"Farwell Pytre, my friend," he said. "I will miss you. Jesus, my Lord, please take care of him." With that he spurred his camel around, and led the caravan to Damascus.

CHAPTER THREE

Wounded in Action

Northeast of Kabul, Afghanistan
2 June 2010

Commander Mike Wayne, Commander of Seal Team Three, called his deputy commander aside after the briefing.

"Curt," he said. "I need you and Samson running point on this one. This is big. We can not have any fuck ups. It is a political nightmare, and also vital to national security. That's why I asked the impossible of you, command Team A and run point."

"Yes sir, Mike," said Lieutenant Curtis Mays, Deputy Commander of Seal Team Three. "So the United States of America, the undisputed masters of weapons of mass destruction, could drop a couple thousand 500 pound block busters on this location, but then we would have to justify that to the world by saying that al-Qaeda had a Soviet lost nuke. So instead we are going to send in a handful of men and a dog. Politically very clean, but if we screw it up, we could end up some time in the future with a nuke terrorist attack in say New York City, or Washington, D.C."

"Yep," said Mike. "Pretty much so, that's it."

"Well sir," said Curt, coming to attention. "You will not find a better dog than Samson, a more competent handler than me, a better team than my A Team, or a better seal team than your Seal Team Three. When it comes to matters of the balance of the free world, you can only depend on us. We will get this job done, and be home by Samson's birthday on the 4th of July."

Mike smiled a sad smile, and nodded toward his office. Curt followed him. Mike closed the door, and said, "I just found out prior to the briefing that Smithy was killed in a terrorist attack in Belgium two months ago. A bomb, that took out most of his dogs. The breeding area was destroyed. It also killed Samson's mom. What was her name?"

"Maw," said Curt. "She sired over one hundred pups. A puppy mill in our country, but Smithy gave her a two acre run, and let her choose her mates." Curt's eyes began to mist. "She was more like a trailer park queen."

Mike laughed. "I'm offended," he said. "As an African American, I would think she was a ghetto queen."

"Sorry Mike," said Curt. "I was forgetting."

"Well, "said Mike. "That's what I love about you. Race doesn't matter. Hell, species doesn't matter. You are a mission person. There is right, and there is wrong. And, you let people live, or you make them die based on them being right or wrong, and nothing else." Mike reached over and gave Curt a hug. It was a deep embrace. "You. Smithy. Well now only just you and I know that Samson was born on 2 June. We are the only ones that know the circumstance of his birth."

"Wow!" Mike said after more reflection. He was mad now. "It is hard to believe that Samson, the undisputed runt of the litter, the dog that was almost stillborn, a dog that was born three days after the other pups of his litter, a dog that should be recognized for his actual birthday, but, the United States Navy says, the Fourth of July is much more patriotic. So that's Samson's official Navy birthday."

"Well," said Curt. "Happy Birthday to Samson! The greatest dog in the world!"

"Here, here," said Mike. Samson entered the room through his special passage door, and sat down on the rug in front of the commander's desk.

Mike opened his refrigerator and pulled out a raw chicken leg. He also grabbed three ice cubes from the top freezer compartment. He put them in a bowl and gave them to Samson.

Samson looked at Curt who said, "Go ahead boy, that little bit won't hurt you before the mission. Happy Birthday my friend."

Samson began to chow down. Mike and Curt sat down on the couch, and watched Samson enjoy his treat in silent reverie. Thirty minutes later they got up, and headed for the equipment room. They all three had to be at the flight line in less than two hours.

The Special Ops Equipped UH-60 Blackhawk helicopter taxied down the runway, and landed at the ready line. This was going to be a short fifteen minute flight, with a fast-rope in. They would be hovering over the LZ for less than twenty seconds. Because of this, Samson was strapped to Curt's back. For a normal repel, Samson would have his own harness. This would have taken longer. The trade off was that now, one of the Seals would have to assist Curt in releasing Samson. Six Seal Team members, including Curt, with Samson strapped to his back, boarded the Blackhawk. Eleven more men waited behind to board the second Blackhawk.

Four minutes later, the copilot radioed, "Half a klick out."

Curt looked at his team, and each one nodded back at him. The Blackhawk flared into a hover, and the men were out of the aircraft. Curt assumed a kneeling ready position while Samson was released. Putting Samson on a lead, the men took off at a fast pace toward their objective.

Samson led the team, zigzagging back and forth. Every now and then he would stop, and sniff the ground or sniff the air. Then he would resume with the silent Team A in close pursuit. Around four kilometers into their journey Samson stopped. His tail went up. First it went into the curved question mark position, and then straight up. Curt went up to Samson; the rest of the team went into a crouched high alert security wedge. Curt nudged Samson. Samson did not budge. This meant that they were close. It was now going to all be up to Samson for the next few moments.

Releasing the lead, Curt said, "Reviere." Samson silently took off like a shot. The men waited.

A few seconds later they heard barking, growling, and human shouts. The men took off at a sprint toward the sounds. Then gunfire, more growling, and human screams. Samson was doing his hit and run tactics, causing great confusion among the enemy.

There was more gunfire, more growling, more shouts, and more human screams. The men were seconds away now. Then there was a semi-burst of gunfire, and a yelp, followed by about three seconds of silence.

"Oh shit," Curt muttered. He burst into a clearing of a make shift compound. There were about a hundred crates of what appeared to be munitions, surrounded by triple strand rolls of concertino wire. In front of that were a tent, and the disturbed remains of a low burning fire. With his optics he could see about a dozen men running around all Helter Skelter. He began picking them off with his double tap system of one to the chest, and one to the head. After dispatching a couple of people he saw the limp form of Samson.

"No," whispered Curt. His optics picked up a heat signature. "Thank you God." Samson was still alive. The delay had caused Curt to be silhouetted for about six seconds. A mistake that was about to cost him dearly.

A machine gun opened up from the side of the compound. The 7.62 mm rounds slammed into Curt's chest knocking him off his feet. As he fell, two rounds entered under his flax vest puncturing his stomach, and intestines. Three more rounds entered his right leg. One of these nicked his femoral artery. He landed hard on his back. As he looked over he saw Samson struggling to raise his head.

There was a "pop-pop" from behind him, and the machine gun went silent. The team was mopping up. They had to secure the area before they could render aid. Team B was about five minutes out. Their mission was to sweep for counter forces, aid Team A in the event they ran into trouble, and to take care of the munitions dump with the suspected tactical nuke after Team A had secured it.

As the team mopped up, a solitary gray bearded man exited the tent. He was wearing a dirty white tunic, and carrying an old 38 caliber revolver in his right hand. The man approached Curt's prone form. Curt looked up at the man. The man snarled, his eyes blazing with hatred. He cocked the hammer on the revolver, aimed it at Curt's head, and muttered something Curt didn't understand. Then the man dropped his gun, screamed, and grabbed at his crotch. Samson was firmly attached by "the bite."

There was a "pop-pop," and the man fell dead to the ground. Only then did Samson release his bite. Samson crawled over to Curt and laid his head on Curt's chest.

A team member kneeled down beside Curt and said, "I need to stop that bleeding sir." Curt could hear a few shots of gunfire in the distance. The team member put direct pressure on Curt's leg. Curt passed out.

Chapter Four

Snakes

Memphis, Egypt
21 March, 29 BC

Four year old Jesus ran up to Mary. "Mom, Mom," he said excitedly. "Can I go play in the river?" The Nile River was about half a mile from their dwelling. It was a favorite spot for the children to play.

Mary looked down affectionately at Jesus. "I suppose," she said. "But take Pytre with you and you mind Pytre now."

"Yes mama," Jesus said, and gave Mary a big hug. He took off out the door. Pytre, without being told, scrambled after him.

Mary watched as the two figures receded into the distance. Joseph came up behind Mary, and wrapped his arms around her. "We are blessed to have that mutt." He joked.

Mary rubbed his hand with her hand. "It is the best gift the Magi gave us," she said.

"And the only one we have left," Joseph said, now serious. It had taken everything they had to flee Judea and set up in Memphis. "But the Lord has always provided us with what we need." Joseph rested his head on Mary's shoulder.

"I truly believe that Pytre is part of that," Mary said. "He is a guardian to ensure that Jesus survives to fulfill his mission on Earth."

"Amen," said Joseph. A tear rolled down his cheek.

* * *

Jesus laughed and twirled around in circles on the river bank. "Look," giggled Jesus, as he held up a sea shell with the critter inside poking his head out. "My father's place is so wonderful." Pytre bounced up and down. His jagged right ear flopping as he moved.

Both boy and dog had a great time playing in the tidal zone. They would chase critters, chase each other, and sometimes Jesus would pick up a stick of drift wood he had found, and throw it down the riverbank. Pytre would go fetch it, and bring it back. Jesus would then throw it a few more times. Pytre liked this part the best. The time flew by. Before any of them had realized it, the new spring sun was starting to set.

"Better head back," said Jesus. He rubbed Pytre's head, and started back toward their house. Pytre fell into step beside Jesus.

About a thousand yards down the trail, the wind stirred, and a bush started moving. It caught Jesus' attention. There was an opening in the rocks behind the bush. Jesus watched fascinated. "Look," Jesus whispered. "A cave." He had never noticed it before. Pytre stiffened and started a low growl. "Come on," Jesus commanded, and took off for the cave. Pytre held firm, and began to bark. Jesus kept running. As the distance closed by half, Pytre took off at a run toward Jesus, still continuing to bark. As Jesus approached the cave, Pytre shot past him, and entered the cave. Jesus came crashing in after him. First thing Jesus noticed was that the floor was moving.

"Yikes," cried Jesus. "Snakes! I have stumbled into a viper den."

Pytre was barking like crazy. He was using his snout and front paws to push back the vipers. Many of them were biting him. As he drove them back, he would shift directions, and use his butt to try and push Jesus out of the cave. Jesus recovered, and stumbled backwards out of the cave. After a few seconds, Pytre emerged. He was staggering, but kept nudging at Jesus. They headed toward the trail. Vipers began slithering out the mouth of the cave, but as boy and dog disappeared, they slithered back into the cave.

Jesus and Pytre collapsed on the trail. Jesus was breathing hard and his heart was racing. Pytre was breathing hard, but labored. His heart began to slow. He had been bitten about twelve times. His heart slowed even more, and then it stopped.

Jesus clutched Pytre up in his tiny arms. "No," he wailed and began to weep. He gave Pytre a hard squeeze. "Please Father!" Jesus said looking upward. Jesus squeezed Pytre again. And Pytre's heart beat, once.

Jesus continued to wail and squeeze Pytre. With each squeeze, Pytre's heart beat. However, his blood was starting to coagulate. He had been bitten before. He had a sort of immunity, but not for this much venom. With each heartbeat, a tear from Jesus feel on Pytre. As Jesus prayed the

Holy Spirit entered the dog. His hemoglobin started to mutate, and Pytre's blood started to thin into a soup. After several minutes of Jesus' extreme grief, Pytre began to breath. He let out a whimper, and licked Jesus' face.

Jesus smiled. He continued to weep, but this time out of joy, not grief. "I love you Pytre," he whispered. "May your days be as numbered as mine?" A nagging thought hit Jesus. He fell silent for a few minutes, and then he whispered, "And may your death be peaceful, regardless of how mine is." They sat there for minutes, boy embracing dog, and the dog licking the boy's face. Finally, Jesus got up. Pytre followed.

"We don't have to tell Mom about this right away," Jesus said. Pytre wagged his tail.

Mary sat on the floor and bit her lower lip. She trusted in the word of God, but she was still a mother, and worrying came natural to all moms. The sun had set and it was starting to get dark. Four year old Jesus had never been late before. Joseph paced up and down the room. "I'm going to tan that boy's hide," said Joseph. Mary just smiled at him. For an old man, he sure does fret like a women, she thought. Joseph continued to nervously pace back and forth. As the sky grew darker, the door pushed open, and a tear streaked Jesus walked into the room, followed by Pytre.

Joseph dropped to his knees. "Thank God," he said, and hugged Jesus tight to him. Mary, who was in the process of getting up, dropped to her knees, and moved over toward the group. She surveyed Jesus intently, and then wrapped her arms around all three of them.

"Its okay, Papa," said Jesus. "I'm okay. Pytre saved me." Joseph reached over and scratched Pytre's head. Mary looked at Jesus sternly, but didn't say anything.

"Snakes mama," Jesus finally said. "Pytre tried to warn me, and he got bit. Several times, but God saved him."

Joseph struggled to his feet. "We've got to get out of this God forsaken land," he exclaimed.

"Hush," said Mary. "They have snakes in Judea. Besides, God will tell us when it is time to go."

"I suppose you're right," said Joseph. He helped Mary to her feet. "Let's eat." Joseph headed to the cooking hearth. They all followed. Pytre was wagging his tail again. Mary served them their bowls of dinner as they sat around the table. Pytre got an extra helping.

* * *

That night Joseph had a dream. In the dream, an angel appeared at the foot of Joseph's bed. In the waking world, Pytre smelled a wonderful fragrance. He looked up and saw a glowing all white magnificent creature that was like a man, only real tall, and had giant wings growing out of his back. Pytre let out a soft whine and wagged his tail. In the dream, the angel spoke to Joseph.

"Soon Joseph," said the Angel in the dream. "Just a couple more years and you may return to your homeland. Until then you must remain here. Your family will be safe."

Joseph's sleeping body became relaxed, and he fell into an even deeper stage of sleep. He did not wake until morning.

CHAPTER FIVE

Trauma Hospital

Kandahar Air Field, Afghanistan
4 June 2010

Curt knew he was dreaming because he was talking with his father, and he had many memories of after his father had died. Still it was pleasant, because he knew it was a dream and not real. He relaxed in the dream.

Curt had just graduated the Navel Academy at Annapolis, Maryland. His dad, Captain Christopher Mays, had pinned on his ensign bars. They were standing on the walkway of the third island of the Chesapeake Bay Bridge Tunnel, looking out over the Chesapeake Bay.

"Son," Captain Mays said. "I am so proud of you. Of course, in Navy talk that means, that's going to cost you. Now you will have to listen as I impart some words of wisdom on you."

Curt smiled and said, "Yes sir Dad."

"I understand you volunteered to go Seal?" His father asked.

"Yes sir," Curt said.

"Tough assignment," His father continued. "I wish you the best of luck. That's harder than my field of submarines." His dad was silent, reflecting on some personal thoughts for a moment. "Anyway," he continued. "There are two frames of mind for Navy leaders. First, if you are in command, you must be of the action frame of mind. That means constant, quick, action activities. Now the draw back to this is, you will find, when in command, is that, you often out distance your brain. When acting rapidly, you can't think that fast, so you will make mistakes. The enemy commander will either do the same, or be slow of action, but that's good. That allows you to win with a lesser plan because you were there first."

"Now," his father continued. "The beauty of the United States Navy, what puts America on the top of the food chain, is the XO." (He pronounced each letter.) "The executive office is of the thinking frame of mind. The obvious draw back is that thinking takes time. That means we have lots of great after action reports on how we could have won, if only we had acted in time."

Curt's dream shifted from memory to translucent. His father changed into the sixty six year old cancer patient he had last seen him as. "Curt," he said, clutching his son with knurled hands. "You were in command of that team. It wasn't your fault."

Curt woke with a start. He was lying in a hospital bed. The first thing he saw was Mike seated in a chair next to his bed. "Sa... Sam….," Curt tried to talk, but his throat was so dry.

Mike leaned over the bed, and whispered, "Samson is okay. However he was shot up almost as bad as you were."

A foreign national orderly came in carrying a medical bag. He sat the bag down beside the bed, and pulled out a blood pressure machine. After taking Curt's blood pressure he said, "146 over 58. Not bad considering your injuries. He pulled out a stethoscope and listened to Curt's chest. "Normal," he said. "Lungs are clear." He grabbed Curt's wrist, stared at the wall clock for about fifteen seconds, nodded, and then left.

"Who was that?" Curt asked in a raspy whisper.

"Don't know that one," said Mike. "But listen up. The mission was a great success. You and Samson were the only casualties, and you two are very much still alive. In fact, if you don't damage yourself any further, you will be back on active duty within two months, tops."

"Good." said Curt. He rolled over toward Mike and felt the stab of something on his cheek. "What's this?" He asked.

"The Navy Commendation Medal, with V device," said Mike. "Plus your Purple Heart."

"What?" Said Curt. He was starting to talk more normally now. "You are giving me a medal for valor for fucking up?"

"You did it bravely," said Mike. "Samson is getting the Bronze Star, with V device, along with his Purple Heart."

"For causing me to screw up," Curt gasped.

"He did it bravely," Mike said with a smile.

"He could care less about medals," Curt said. "Hell, he doesn't even have a place to pin them on. What Samson would really like is a raw, plucked, and cleaned chicken."

"You spoil that dog with to many treats," Mike said, pretending sternest. "You are going to make that dog fat."

"What if I just give him a chicken leg on his birthday," Curt joked. "And a whole raw chicken, only when he saves my life?"

"I suppose that's okay," grinned Mike. Then more seriously he said. "The mission was a great success. We recovered an old Soviet tactical nuke warhead, no delivery system, no detonation system, but it could have made a very nasty dirty bomb. You probably saved the lives of a million plus people. We also recovered several hundred boxes of 7.62 millimeter ammunition." Mike grinned. "Probably would have been a lot more if you and Samson wouldn't have hogged so many rounds for yourself."

"Damn it sir," sighed Curt. "Show some mercy."

Mike gently patted Curt on his shoulder. "I'm so very proud of you my friend," he said. "Oh, I've got a treat for you. Samson is up and moving around. He is on his way to see you. I'll go get him." Mike got up from his chair, and headed out the door. As Mike closed the door behind him, he saw the elevator door open, and Samson, being led by Nurse Amy, who among many qualifications was also a very qualified dog handler, exited the elevator.

At that moment, the sixty percent Potassium Chlorate IED (Improvised Explosive Device) in the medical bag beside Curt's bed exploded.

The explosion flung Curt's bed, with Curt on it, into the wall and, the door that Mike had just closed. The heavy hospital bed shielded Curt from most of the blast, but the impact with the wall was severe. The wounds in his stomach and intestines were reopened. The impact with the wall also cracked three of his ribs, fractured his right Zygomatic bone, just under his eye, and caused serious trauma to his right knee. As if his problems weren't enough, his room was on fire, and rapidly filling with smoke. Curt's bed was on fire. A diagonal section of the door about three feet wide had blown out. Smoke was billowing into the hallway. The sprinkler system in Curt's room went off. Smoke detector alarms were going off everywhere. They competed in the confusion with a loud siren. The base was going on lockdown. Curt was on the floor, but a thick layer of acrid smoke was filling the room. He had to get out of there, but he was wedged in the debris.

The furry head and forepaws of Samson appeared at the hole in the door. Samson paused for a second to scan the room, and then scurried through the opening into Curt's room. Samson began dragging the charred hospital bed and other debris away from Curt, and away from the door. Mike's head kept appearing at the hole in the door as he jumped up and down trying to peer in. Samson stood over Curt for a second, whined, licked Curt's face, and then bit the front of his hospital gown and dragged him away from the door. Mike opened the door, coughing on the smoke, crouched down, and dragged Curt out of the room.

In the corridor, controlled mayhem was playing out. Doctors, Nurses, Orderlies, Security, Firemen, and patients were rapidly moving in all directions. The over pressurized atmosphere of the building was causing the smoke to reenter Curt's room, and exit the building thru the blown out window and partial wall on the opposite side of the room. Curt laid against the far wall a couple of feet from the elevators. He was surrounded by the kneeling figures of Mike and a trauma doctor. Samson sat rigid next to Curt, facing the crowd, scanning for threats. Nurse Amy stood next to Samson. She gentle stroked his head with her burn scared hands. Samson licked her hand. Nurse Amy's main mission was to keep Samson from attacking some well meaning orderly or fireman whom Samson might perceive as a threat.

The doctor was asking Curt all kinds of questions, making him wiggle his toes, and move various body parts. Curt looked over at Mike whose face was etched in deep anguish. Curt gave his friend a huge smile.

"Okay," Curt said. "I won't give him a whole chicken every time he saves my life. Hell, he'd weigh three hundred pounds before his next birthday." Mike burst out laughing.

Chapter Six

Chasing Birds

Nazareth, Galilee
2 June, 21 BCE

Twelve year old Jesus played in the streambed. He silhouetted Mount Tabor which rose in splendor to the east of Jesus. Pytre rolled on his back in a tuff of grass under a walnut tree up on the west bank. He rocked back in forth, kicking his paws up in the air. His tongue lolled out the side of his mouth, and he had a big smile on his face. Pytre was totally in the moment.

Jesus stopped playing, and watched Pytre. He loved and was awed by all of his father's creations, but Pytre, the dog, was his favorite. He likened dogs in par with humans and, Pytre was his best friend. Jesus thought of how Pytre loved to fetch things. Suddenly Jesus got an idea.

"Pytre," Jesus called. Pytre stopped rolling and got up. Jesus reached into the clay bottom of the stream he was standing in and scooped up some of the mud. He formed it in his hands into a sparrow. Holding it to his face he breathed on it. The clay sparrow came to life. Jesus tossed the bird into the air. "Fetch," Jesus said. The bird took off about two feet off the ground and flew west, almost straight at Pytre, but then swerved about ten yards away. Pytre took off after the bird. As the bird flew, he began to climb in altitude. At ten yards he was two and a half feet up in the air. At twenty yards he was three feet in altitude. Pytre calculated the bird's flight. This was fun. This was invigorating. Pytre ran a triangular course, and at forty yards out leaped high into the air and caught the sparrow. He chomped down on the bird and fell the six feet back to earth. When he hit ground, the bird had transformed into a stick of driftwood. Pytre brought the stick back to Jesus.

"Good boy," beamed Jesus. He touched the stick, and it turned into a savory meat treat. Pytre gobbled it down. Jesus laughed.

Jesus reached into the stream bed and grabbed another handful of mud. He fashioned another sparrow, breathed life into it, and flung it into the air. Pytre took off after it. This bird made an arcing semi circle glide path toward the north. Pytre calculated the trajectory, and sprinted off on an intercepting course. The bird climbed in altitude, but made sine wave type dipping movements. Pytre leaped into the air, and caught the bird on a dip at about eight feet off the ground. He tumbled back to Earth, but kept the bird tightly clenched in his jaw. He had leaped almost quadruple his height. When he hit the ground he rolled. The stick of driftwood remained in his grasp. He brought it back to Jesus who rewarded him with a savory meat treat.

Boy and dog played like that for several hours. Jesus was happy. Pytre was experiencing the most rewarding, satisfying, and fulfilling time of his life. To the outsider witnessing this game, it might have seemed impossible, or at least miraculous. However, Pytre took it all in stride, living for the moment, enjoying the moment. What master did was okay with him. After all, that was why he was master. All things were possible. Life was now. Life was to be lived now. Life was to be enjoyed. He was dog.

As the sun lowered, boy and dog retreated to under the walnut tree. Jesus lay with his back against the trunk. Pytre snuggled up next to him. He licked his hair and the side of his neck and face. Jesus laughed.

"This has been a wonderful day," said Jesus. Pytre wagged his tail in agreement. "I declare this day, in my Father's name, as Dog Appreciation Day. It is seventy-two days from the Spring Equinox and nineteen days until the Summer Solstice. It shall hereafter be a day of bonding between man and dog." Pytre bounced up and down, licking Jesus' face.

Jesus got up and headed back to his home. Pytre heeled by his side. As they approached the dwelling, Pytre veered off to the right, circled the house, making stops to sniff the area. Jesus entered through the door. Pytre, having made his perimeter check, entered the house a few seconds after Jesus.

"Welcome home Jesus," said Mary. She was standing at the cooking hearth stirring a pot of something that smelled delicious.

"Hi Mom," said Jesus, giving her a hug. She fixed him a steaming bowl of goat stew. He took the bowl and sat on the floor at the table. Mary carried two more bowls to the table. She set one in front of Joseph, and the other one on the floor in front of Pytre. Mary fixed another bowl for herself and joined them at the table. Joseph gave the blessing.

A snoring sound could be heard. They all looked at Pytre who was sound asleep in front of his untouched supper bowl. Mary and Joseph looked at Jesus.

"What?" Jesus said. "I feed him some treats today, and he's had a lot of exercise." Mary smiled and shook her head. Joseph chuckled. Pytre continued to lightly snore. He was having a wonderful dream about chasing birds.

CHAPTER SEVEN

The Meeting

San Diego, California
2 June 2011

After clearing security, Curt entered the briefing room. He was wearing his Navy camouflage uniform. He carried a cardboard box. Samson came in behind him, his lead trailing on the ground. Curt sat the box on the table.

Mike stood up and extended his hand. "Good to see you again Curt," said Mike. "And you too Samson." Samson wagged his tail. Mike glanced at his watch. "It's 2200 hours. Considering we are in orange cycle, I'm glad we all could make it on such short notice. Your phone call really intrigued me." Mike glanced around the room. "I know you haven't seen us in a while, but you know these guys. We got the Chief, and your old assistant, my acting deputy, Lieutenant George Smith. We also have Captain Dustin Martinez from Navel Intelligence." Curt shook his hand. "And Fred, from the CIA."

"Fred," said Curt. "It's been about five years."

"Yes," said Fred. "Last time I saw you it was in Iraq. I was the one shot up then. It's good to see you again." Fred shook Curt's hand.

"Small world," said Mike. "Will everybody please be seated?" The group sat down around the oval shaped table. "Curt has been on convalescent leave since he was discharged from Walter Reed four months ago," Mike continued. "He and Samson were shot up pretty bad exactly a year ago today. Two days after that, they tried to finish the job with an IED. This afternoon Curt calls me with a very bizarre tale. Way to many coincidences for my liking. Curt please recap that for us."

24

"Today Samson and I went to a dog friendly place called *Rock Hounds*. It is Samson's birthday. Until today, I thought only Commander Wayne and I were the only two that knew that. Smithy, Samson's Breeder was killed a little over a year ago. Samson's mom, Maw, gave birth to a litter of eight pups on 30 May 2006. She remained sick and feverish for three days. Then on 2 June 2006, she gave birth to Samson, the obvious runt of the litter. Samson didn't look like he was going to make it, but within a week he was the strongest, toughest, and most intelligent of the litter. Maw seemed to like him best. Mike, uhhh, Commander Wayne and I were at the farm recruiting pups when Samson was born. I took an instant shine to him. Within a week I, we, had developed a strong bond to each other. I don't think it was rigged." Curt glanced at Mike sheepishly. "But four months later, I picked Samson's number from the hat. When I entered the kennel, of course all the other dogs were going wild. The noise was deafening. I had number six two. As I approached cage sixty-two, Samson was just sitting there, as if he was expecting me. We have been a team ever since." Curt paused. Samson cocked his head and looked at Curt encouragingly.

"Today," Curt continued. "A man who identified himself only as Pytre, a very strange looking man, knew Samson, and at least knew his true birthday and that he had been shot with an AK-47. Even scarier, Samson appeared to know him. A horrible thought crossed my mind. Smithy was killed by the IRA. The beef against me has been from al-Qaeda. What if they have teamed up in some unholy alliance?"

"Why," asked Senior Master Chief Gary Owen, "would a Catholic group team up with a Muslim group?"

"Why," asked Fred, "did the Nazis, a racist Aryan group, allied themselves with the Japanese, a racist Oriental group? In fact, the Nazis killed Aryan enemies for the Japanese, while the Japanese killed oriental enemies for the Nazis. Politics make strange bed fellows."

"This is bad news." Chief said, "Pretty scary shit."

"Amen," said Curt. "Sir, you have the surveillance tapes?"

Mike reached under the table and pulled out a drawer with a keyboard on it. "Watch this," he said. He typed some things on the keyboard. "Curt sent me this from the surveillance tapes at *Rock Hounds*." They all watched the video in stunned silence.

When it was over, Captain Martinez said, "Only three cameras, there are lots of gaps, but he doesn't appear on camera until he sits at the table. How did he enter the café?"

"Wow, he loves his milk," Fred said. "But, he also exits the café the same way he entered. He walks off camera two, and does not reappear on camera one."

"Curt," said Captain Martinez. "How much coverage gap do you think there is between the cameras?"

"My guess, sir," said Curt. "It is not more that a swath of maybe three feet wide by twenty feet long, and it's all out in the open."

"Interesting," said Captain Martinez. "That's a concrete patio for the whole area?"

"Yes sir," said Curt.

They were slowly playing the video again for the third time. This time they were stopping, pausing, and reversing the tape, while taking notes, and asking questions.

"Curt," said Captain Martinez. "Any alerts in the rowdy crowd of drunks?"

"No sir," said Curt. "All of them regulars of at least a year. That makes them prior to me. Sam and Karen have given me their identities and addresses. Hey they run a tab." Curt reached into the box he had brought with him and took out a folder.

"Chief," said Mike, taking the folder from Curt, and handing it to his Master Chief.

"On it sir," said the Chief.

"Hold it," said Fred. "Play that scene right there again." The tape was reversed and replayed. "Curt," asked Fred. "Is Seal Team Six really your favorite Seal Team?" The room erupted in laughter.

"Shut the hell up Fred," said Curt. He was shaking his head, but it was a needed break from the tension. The CIA, once again, to the rescue with some light hearted humor, thought Curt.

The film advanced to the drunken group at Pytre's table. Captain Martinez stopped the film from the console at his seat. "Okay," he said. "Smithy seems to be the link. Nobody knows it is Samson's birthday. If you hacked into any files, you would discover that the fourth of July is his birthday. But! Look at Pytre's mannerism. His body language states sincerity, even utmost honesty. Could he be an idiot savant that worked with Smithy? What hard evidence do you have?"

Curt moved to the box, and started pulling out evidence. "Fingerprint cards I did on Karen and Sam," he said as he handed them to Captain Martinez. "This," he said. "Is the meal of Pytre; plate of ribs, glass of milk, pitcher of milk, tablecloth, napkin, and unused silverware. Also a plastic bag containing eight gnawed rib bones, plus four, uneaten ones. There will be DNA on those. I hope we can find a match."

Captain Martinez took the box. "You got the NSA and Navel Intelligence running this. If Pytre is anywhere in the system, we will find him," said Martinez. "Anybody have any theories on this?"

"Well," said Fred, leaning forward in his chair. "I believe in coincidences, but I don't accept them until all other possibilities have been disproved. I say we approach this first as an unholy alliance conspiracy, then look at terrorist groups acting alone, and then small group or individuals acting alone. I mean, if we are going to stop a combined effort by our enemies to bring down the American giant," he paused. "That will be every body's top priority, but," Fred continued. "If this does turn out to be just some animal rights group that is only trying to wish Samson a happy birthday, it is not such a priority. However, a person or group this proficient needs to come on our radar, just in case their ideology changes in the future."

"I agree," said Captain Martinez. "I will be kept in the loop please."

Mike stood up. "So we all have our work cut out for us," he said. "Are we done?" He looked at Fred. Fred nodded. Then at Captain Martinez who also nodded. "Seal Team Three?" They all nodded as he looked at them except for Samson, who cocked his head and wagged his tail. "Well, until next time, Trident Canine Warriors!" All of Seal Team Three jumped to their feet, even Samson.

"All the way and then some more," they said in unison. Samson barked once.

"Dismissed," said Mike.

"Curt," Mike continued as everyone left the room except for Fred and Captain Martinez. "We are officially keeping you on convalescent leave, however we are assigning you to this case. You might want to think about growing a beard, maybe even letting your hair grow long. Anyway, we meet back here in a couple of days." Mike handed Curt a BO7 cell phone. "I'll let you know."

Curt took the phone and said, "Thanks, I'll comb every dog park in the area. I'll see you in a couple of days."

Chapter Eight

The Sermon on the Bank

Jordan River, Galilee
2 June 3 BCE

Pytre rose from his crouch, and leaped into the stream. He surfaced a moment later with the fish in his mouth and paddled back to shore. Lady, his wife, watched admiringly from shore. Three of his sons gave each other knowing glances. Their dad was the best hunter in the world. Lady limped over to Pytre and took the fish from his mouth. She was getting old. She was fifteen. She marveled at Pytre. He was old when she met him twelve years ago. He was mourning the loss of his wife then. She had died old and content, but Pytre still lived on. What an amazing mate she had.

Pytre gestured with his head and the three oldest boys followed him over to the bank. They all crouched. Pytre tapped Malika, his first born by Lady, who watched intently. When Pytre lifted his paw off Malika, he leaped into the water. When Malika surfaced the water he had a fish in his mouth. He had caught it by the tail. The fish whapped against Malika repeatedly, but Malika held on. The fish hit him on the right front flank, and Malika went down beneath the water. He came up sputtering, but the fish was still in his mouth, this time he had him in the center of the back. He proudly walked to the bank with the fish in his mouth. He strutted around on the bank receiving the admiring glances of his siblings, and dropped the fish on the bank. The fish flapped a few times making it back to the water, and swam away. Malika looked on in chagrinned horror. Pytre smiled. They could have used the meat, but the lesson was probably of more value.

Malika walked over to his father with his head bowed. Pytre lightly cuffed him with his paw. Malika dropped his head lower. Pytre moved back to the bank and called his three boys back over. Malika slowly returned to his position. Pytre put his paw back on Malika, and Malika beamed with pleasure, he had been forgiven. When Pytre lifted his paw, Malika leaped into the water. Malika had not been paying full attention, he had been concentrating on his father's circumspection, so he was only able to grab the fish by the tail, and this one was larger than the last one that he had lost. He bit hold with his front teeth and took up the fight.

"Pytre," Jesus called. All ears went up. It was their master calling. Pytre looked around at his pack, and then took off toward the voice. Pytre gave one bark as he ran, and all the pack, his immediate six, wife, plus three sons, and two daughters followed suit. They all gave a bark, one bark, and thirty-seven other packs, six of Pytre's children's pack, fifteen of his grandchildren's pack, fourteen of his great grandchildren's pack, and two of his great-great grandchildren's pack all took off toward the voice.

Jesus sat down on a rock at the side of the trail on top of the ridge overlooking the riverbank. Pytre broke from the underbrush and leaped on Jesus' lap. He began licking Jesus' face, as Jesus scratched the side of Pytre's head.

"Pytre, my friend," Jesus said as he continued to scratch the side of Pytre's head. Pytre laid his head on his master's chest. "I must go away to complete my teachings. I will not return here in this life." Pytre let out a whimper. "However," Jesus continued. "You will be with me when I die, and you will accompany me when it is time to go to heaven." Pytre looked up and licked the side of Jesus' neck. "It is time for me to say my goodbyes. Please assemble the pack."

Pytre gave out a long, low whine, and then a sharp bark. Two hundred sixteen dogs began to emerge from the underbrush. They all gathered around Jesus on the trail. Some sat, some lay down, but they all were attentive on their master. All of their ears were perked up. The last to enter the trail was Malika. He held a large fish in his mouth. Malika brought the fish to Jesus.

"Thank you Malika," said Jesus. He took the fish, held it in both hands, looked to heaven, and blessed the fish. The fish shimmered with an incandescent glow, and sort of, jerkified into a more malleable substance.

Jesus broke off a large chunk and gave it to Pytre. Pytre ate the chunk of fish in reverence. He was full. Jesus broke off another chuck and gave it to Pytre. Pytre carried it over to his immediate pack. He bit it into pieces and then gave Lady, Malika, and his four remaining children a piece. They ate it and were content.

Jesus nodded and thirty-seven other pack leaders approached him. They each took a chunk from Jesus, and brought it back to their pack. All dogs ate, all were satisfied.

Jesus looked on with approval. "My friends," he said. "I must leave, and you will not see me again in this world." Howls and whines went up from around the packs. Jesus held his hands up for silence. In a few seconds, all dogs had calmed down. Jesus smiled, dogs were like that. So trusting, and living in the moment.

"I would like to say my farewells to you," Jesus continued. "I must go do my teachings to the humans, your masters." Jesus' face clouded in anger. "But they are only masters through God's will. When they abuse that privilege, they will be your enemies. You will defend the children. You will defend the innocent. You will defend those of the pack."

Jesus paused for a moment. He looked upward and closed his eyes. His body relaxed as a peace fell over him. All dogs watched him intently.

"Doggies," he said while opening his eyes, and looking out at them. All tails wagged through out Pytre's clan. "You are all special in the eyes of God," Jesus continued in an upbeat voice. "You are tasked as companions to man. You will serve them. You will comfort them. You will assist them. You will love them, but most importantly, you will accept their love for you. That is very important." All tails wagged. They all understood. Not through language, but through communication. Jesus turned more somber.

"Amongst you," he said. "If a pack member offends you, first go to that pack member to resolve it. If it still can't be resolved, bring it to the other canine pack members. If it still can't be resolved, then, and only then, bring it to your human master. What he decides you must accept unless it goes against the will of God." Jesus paused and smiled.

"Don't eat a lot of sugar," Jesus said. "Worms are a problem, so try to stay away from soft dirt and decayed food that could be infected with worms like buried pork or day old rats. Fish are good for you, but not if they have been lying on the bank or have flukes on them. Use common sense. However, I know that mission may easily get convoluted in the future. So I say unto you here. It is not what a dog eats or receives that makes him bad. No, it is what he does that makes him bad. Be good dogs!"

There were howls and yips, and lots of tail wagging. Jesus smiled. He enjoyed the moment for a while. Finally he said, "Out of my heart flows the spirit of living water. The world can not hate you through following my teachings, but by only hating me for judging their works as evil. You will be of my pack, and my pack is the way to evolve to the next level." The clan of Pytre let out a tremendous howl. "Finally," Jesus said. "Unless a seed falls and dies as itself, it will never grow or bear fruit. So I want you to be real.

Be the salt. Live your life in the present, but also be the light. You don't hide a light under a barrel, you let it shine. Let your deeds be seen. Let humans appreciate what you do through your actions. Let them see your salt. Be both salt and light. I will not see you again in this world. Love each other and love man. I will see you on the next level."

As the dogs howled and returned to the wilderness, Jesus motioned for Pytre and Malika to stay behind.

"Malika," Jesus said, stroking his head. "You are Pytre's oldest, under Lady. Your own wife, Cindy, died a couple of years ago. Your whelps are all grown and have their own packs. You have returned to your father and mother's pack." Malika hung his head. Jesus gently reached under his jaw and lifted his head so that their eyes would meet. "You are the namesake of your dad's second human master. Cy your oldest half sibling, being the namesake briefly, of the first. You are a great dog, a good dog, which honors your namesake and your family. You have had a hard life, but you make us all proud." Pytre looked at his son with tremendous pride.

"I will call your father to me in three years," Jesus continued, still holding Malika by his lower jaw. "At that time you will become the clan leader of all the packs. Until that time, learn as much as you can from your dad." Jesus released Malika's jaw.

They all sat looking at each other for a few moments. Jesus scratched Malika on the top of his head. Finally Jesus nodded, and Malika walked off toward the river and the others. Pytre sat rigidly, looking between Jesus and Malika. Jesus turned toward Pytre and grabbed his head with both hands, ruffling his ears.

"Pytre," Jesus said, still scratching Pytre's ears. "You must train them all well. You must be the example. When I leave today, my influence will leave with me. It will be up to you to keep them on the path." Jesus paused, he started to weep. "I would love to have you stay here, but when I meet my destiny on the cross, I will not be able to stop you from coming to my aide. I love you Pytre." Jesus gave Pytre a big hug. "I will see you in three years."

Jesus got up, grabbed his staff, and walked away. Pytre sat and watched him until he had completely disappeared down the trail. Pytre remained watching the empty trail for many more moments. Then slowly, reluctantly, Pytre got up and disappeared into the underbrush.

CHAPTER NINE

The Meeting Number Two

San Diego, California
5 June 2011

Curt and Samson were already in the briefing room when the others showed up. Mike and Captain Martinez were the last to enter. Mike sat to the right of center, and Captain Martinez sat in the center seat, the chairman's seat. Curt looked at Mike questioningly.

"Let's get started," said Captain Martinez. "Due to recent developments, Navel Intelligence has taken command of this operation. It now has an official name, Project Pytre Dawg. That's Dawg, capital D, a, w, g. It's Pytre's last name. Pytre was born on 2 June 1956 to a couple of carnival sideshow freaks in Norfolk, Virginia. Their names were John and Ethel Dawg, but they were better known as Dog Man and Dog Girl. Their youngest child, Pytre, no middle name, Dawg was completely hairless, and had a skin pigmentation disorder. Pytre was billed as the Son of Dog, the Amazing Human Puppy."

There were murmurs around the room. Captain Martinez paused for a few seconds. "Here is where it gets really interesting," Captain Martinez continued. "No school records on Pytre. Apparently he never attended school. Not that uncommon in those days for people of lower social economic abilities. He next comes on the radar as a twelve year old boy, a mental patient at Norfolk General Hospital. In an amazing bit of luck, we were able to find his old records. These included an envelope with his personal effects. From a tooth brush we were able to match up his DNA as a perfect match with our Pytre, the rib eater of a few days ago." More murmurs around the room. Captain Martinez nodded to Mike, who typed some things on his keyboard. Two pictures appeared on the wall.

"We also found," said Captain Martinez. "His autopsy report, complete with this photo." More murmurs and some gasps from around the table.

"That's impossible," said Curt shaking his head. He was having great difficulty reconciling the black and white photo of the young lad on the table, his chest cut open, many of his organs removed to include his heart, with the man he had met at the café. But the markings on the skin were dead on. This boy on the slab, matched up perfectly with what he had seen of Pytre at the restaurant. This included the deep gash around his neck. The difference being that the boy on the slabs wound was fresh. Curt's head was reeling. He lived in the very real world of logic and science. This made absolutely no sense to him.

When the group had settled down a bit, Captain Martinez continued with his briefing. He nodded to Mike. The autopsy report disappeared and an admittance form appeared. "Pytre Dawg was institutionalized at Norfolk General on 4 June, 1968 by the orders of District Judge Harvey Oats, currently deceased. The reasons stated were acute delusions. In the remarks it states that young Pytre believed himself to be the reincarnation of Jesus Christ's personal dog. It also notes violent tendencies, especially when it came to the defense of dogs. Also note that it records his parents as both deceased. We haven't been able to find the records on this, but apparently our young Pytre had been living as a homeless orphan on the streets of Norfolk for a little while before coming to the attention of the government." Captain Martinez nodded at Mike again and the admittance form was replaced by a counseling report. The autopsy photograph remained up.

"A Doctor Frank Rowell, Psychiatrist, did a thirty day evaluation of our young Pytre on 5 July 1968," Captain Martinez continued. "Dr. Rowell is also currently deceased. In his report of almost forty-three years ago he states that Pytre firmly believes he is the reincarnated dog of Jesus Christ, who also was named Pytre. According to Pytre Dawg, Jesus' dog Pytre, lived to be thirty-three years old. This would be a remarkable longevity record for a dog both today, and in the time of Jesus. We are not aware of any biblical or scholarly records indicating Jesus ever had a dog, by any name. Dr. Rowell gives four monthly reports on Pytre Dawg up until Pytre's murder on 8 November."

Captain Martinez nods again at Mike who flashes the reports up on the screens around the room. He also puts the autopsy report back up. The men get up and study the reports. After several minutes, Fred is the first to speak.

"It seems," said Fred. "That our Dr. Rowell was not making any progress with our Mr. Pytre Dawg. In fact, it looks like young Pytre was having an effect on the good doctor. These last two reports, reading between the lines, would indicate that Dr. Rowell was having second thoughts about Pytre being delusional."

"Well," said Captain Martinez. "Let's look at the autopsy report on the murder. Cause of death is affixation by a picture wire taken from the painting in the recreation room by a Mr. John Doe, age approximately thirty, who strangled young Pytre while he was sleeping. Nothing is known about this John Doe other than he arrived at the ninth floor of Norfolk General as a homeless transient a couple of months before. He believed he was possessed by a demon."

Curt sat down. "Help me out here," he said. "You know I hate all this magic voodoo hoodoo crap. There has got to be a reasonable explanation for all this. Have we exhumed the body?"

"He was cremated," said Captain Martinez. "No clue where the ashes are. Probably swept up and thrown away. He had no friends or family."

"A couple of possible theories I'll throw out," said Fred. "Okay, this story happens around half a century ago. We are in the cold war. Records are sketchy. My number one thought is that it's twins. Not highly probable, but at least possible that Pytre was born twins, and there is no record of the second birth."

Curt began to relax some. His stomach had been tied up in knots since the briefing began. "That would explain the DNA" Curt said.

"And," said Fred "The skin disorder matching so well. It doesn't account for the identical scars, but they could have been added later. That's my favorite theory."

"You have other theories?" Asked Captain Martinez.

"Well," said Fred. "All or some of the documents could be forged and or planted. This doesn't fit in well with Occam's razor, or what I like to call the simplicity factor. Someone would have to go to a lot of trouble to prove a man's death when it would be so simple to erase the proof of his existence instead. We only have the one birth certificate to prove Pytre Dawg ever existed until he shows up in a Psych Ward at age twelve where he is soon to be murdered. It does not make sense to go to all that trouble to fake his death. Of course we may be missing some key elements of this puzzle. This one has me interested."

There were nods and mummers of agreement from all around the room. Captain Martinez raised his hands for silence. "Well," Martinez said. "Other than appearing out of nowhere, knowing things he shouldn't know, and being documented as dead, this guy hasn't done anything wrong. Anymore theories before we continue?"

Fred raised his hand. He had a smirk on his face. "Of course," said Fred. "He could be the reincarnated son of dog who doesn't let death slow him down like us regular mortals." The room burst into laughter, except for Curt. He had a renewed twinge of panic.

"That's not funny," said Curt angrily. "We need to stay focused on the facts." Both Mike and Fred gave Curt a concerned look. "Surely there was a trial for John Doe," continued Curt, ignoring the looks of concern. "What do we have on why he killed him?"

Captain Martinez gave a sigh, and pointed to Mike. Mike typed some commands on his keyboard. The screens went blank. After a few moments, two screens popped up. One was a black and white photograph of a mutilated looking man on a medical slab. The other was another autopsy report.

"John Doe," said Captain Martinez. "Never stood trial or was even charged in the death of Pytre Dawg. On the afternoon following the morning of Pytre's murder, John Doe was being transported to the police station for questioning by two officers and a hospital orderly. He was savagely attacked and killed by a pack of dogs. Neither the police officers nor the orderly were harmed."

Curt's head reeled, and then everything went dark as he crashed to the floor.

Curt became aware of a whining sound in his ear. He opened his eyes. He was lying on his back on the conference room floor. Mike was leaning over him pushing a pillow under his head. Samson was licking the side of his face. Fred was putting some pillows under his feet.

"You okay?" Mike asked. He was now shining a pen light into the sides of Curt's eyes. Curt nodded and tried to get up. Mike held a restraining hand on Curt's chest. "Not so fast my friend," Mike said in a soothing voice. "Let's just lay still for a while." Mike and Fred quickly checked Curt's vitals. The rest of the group had gathered around them. Fred looked at Mike and nodded. "I can help you to the chair if you feel like you're up to it," Mike said to Curt, putting an arm around him. Curt allowed himself to be helped into his chair.

"I must have fainted," said Curt. He felt very embarrassed. This whole Pytre affair had him spooked. He would rather face a battalion of armed terrorist any day over one supernatural entity. "I'm okay now," Curt said. He looked around the room. "Sorry guys. I guess I'm still not completely over my injuries."

"Have him fully checked out Mike," Captain Martinez said to Commander Mike Wayne.

"Yes sir," said Mike. Mike looked over to Curt who nodded.

"Fred," said Captain Martinez. "I like your twin theory, but let's get the facts first. I'm sending you to Norfolk to link up with my teams there. It's a cold trail, but we are the best. Pytre Dawg was born a little over fifty-five years ago. He was murdered a little under forty-three years ago. We need witnesses. Any information is good information. Check out John Doe thoroughly also."

"Yes sir," said Fred.

"Seal Team Three," Captain Martinez continued. "Pytre was last seen here three days ago. Leave no stone unturned."

"Yes sir," said Mike. There were nods and yes sirs from around the room.

"I will send a team to Belgium to check out Smithy's old operation," Captain Martinez continued. "I will also have my internet gurus checking out anything remotely connected on the web. Good luck gentlemen. We will meet back here at 1800 hours on the tenth of June. Dismissed."

Everybody leaped to their feet as Captain Martinez exited the conference room. Fred followed him out. Mike began passing out assignments.

"Curt," Mike said. "Full medical first thing in the morning, then over to *Rock Hounds*. If you meet this guy again, restrain him as legally as you can, but retain him at all cost."

"Yes sir," said Curt. He and Samson left the conference room.

Fred was waiting for them at the elevator. "You okay?" Fred asked. "I know you hate ghost and goblins more than anything else."

"I'm fine Fred," Curt said. "Besides, we will figure this out, and it won't be a ghost or a goblin."

"Okay," said Fred. He patted Curt's arm. "You're the toughest man I know. I will never forget Iraq. If you need anything just let me know."

"Thanks my friend," said Curt. "I will never forget Iraq either. Besides, there are no such things as ghost." Fred got on the elevator, and waited. Curt and Samson entered. As the elevator closed Curt thought, I've just got to convince myself of that.

CHAPTER TEN

Crucifixion

Calvary, Jerusalem
0 BCE/0 AD

Pytre had been traveling non stop for three days now. His master, Jesus, had summoned him. He would not be going back. In preparation he had left Malika in charge of the whole clan. Each pack leader was strong, and able to lead their pack in survival. Malika would strengthen them as a team. They would probably all stay together for a year or two, and then they would slowly split off into their own separate packs. Pytre had made his farewells. He knew he would not see them again until the beyond, but he also knew that they would all have a happy healthy life.

"My friend," Jesus' soothing voice resounded in Pytre's conscious. "I sure miss the comfort of your company." Pytre could feel the loving arms of his master around him. They were slick, and Pytre could smell Jesus' blood, sweat, and tears on them. Pytre gave a renewed burst of energy, and headed for his master's location.

As Pytre broke through the underbrush into the clearing, he came upon a squad of Roman soldiers.

"Dinner has arrived," shouted Casca, a member of the squad. Laughing, he grabbed his short sword and cracked Pytre hard across the face. Pytre staggered and fell over on his left side. Blood squirted from the gash. A nasty uppercut wound that went from his left cheek, across his nose, barely missing is right eye, and exiting out the right side of his forehead.

Pytre slowly got up. Letting out a low growl he faced his attacker. Pytre kept constant eye contact with Casca as the two opponents circled each other.

"You're a tough one," said Casca. "I like that. Maybe you won't be dinner." A horse came up behind Pytre. Pytre kept his gaze on Casca. The man was the greater threat.

Casca raised his hand and said, "I got this Sarge. This is one strong dog. Maybe we should just let him go about his business."

A noose dropped over Pytre's head. It tightened, and Pytre was hoisted into the air. "You are such a loser," said Sergeant Sporus. He flung Pytre over the back of his horse. "You will always be a loser Casca," Sporus continued.

Casca glowered with unbridled hatred at Sergeant Sporus. The Sarge had been riding his ass since the Legion got to Judea over six months ago. Sporus looked at him, laughed, turned his horse, and rode off toward the main camp. Pytre bounced on the back of the horse. The noose was cutting into his neck with every bounce. About twenty strides toward the main camp Sergeant Sporus wheeled the horse around and shouted. "Casca, you stupid son of a bitch, when I'm done having my fun with this mutt, you are going to kill it, butcher it, and serve it to me for dinner. If you don't, if it is not cooked properly, then your weekend pass is cancelled, and you will be serving extra duty." With a laugh Sporus spun the horse back toward main camp, and took off at a gallop. Casca scowled at the retreating figures.

Sergeant Sporus galloped into the main camp. He rode up to the cooking hearth and slung Pytre in front of the fire. "I don't care what you do to this mutt," said Sporus. "Just don't kill him. That job will be left up to that no good son of a bitch Casca. I will return to summon him in four hours. Make sure the dog is still alive when I do." Sporus trotted off toward Jerusalem. He had a date.

The men slowly got up, and surrounded the dog. Pytre, after three days of travel and all the blood loss, was too weak to get up. He just lay still, accepting whatever fate was to be his. The men looked down on him.

"He isn't going to make it," said one. "What do we do? I don't want Sergeant Sporus mad at me."

"Put him in the cage," said the cook, an old German man. "His fate, like ours, is in the hands of the gods."

"The one true God," muttered the Syrian Jew under his breath. He was new to the Legion, and therefore the lowest ranking. He grabbed Pytre, and dragged him to the cage. He removed the lanyard and carried him into the cage, a six foot high structure made of tree branches lashed together. It currently housed eight goats, twelve lambs, and fourteen pigs. He laid Pytre in the corner of the cage. One of the lambs came over and sniffed Pytre, then walked off. The other animals left Pytre alone. Satisfied, the legionnaire left Pytre, closed and latched the cage, and headed back to the rest of the men. Pytre slept. In his mind he could feel his master stroking his head.

* * * * *

Casca had been alternating between leaning against a tree and angrily pacing the field since Sporus had left. He was seething with rage. Who the hell did Sporus thing he was. Casca was also a Roman. He was a free citizen. He had volunteered for service to do his duty and escape the ghetto he had been born and raised in on the outskirts of Rome. Casca would be a Sergeant one day, if he were lucky enough to live. He might even be an officer. All he needed was some lucky breaks and a little education. Casca fanaticized about outranking Sporus. The things he would do to that man. This made him feel a little better. With a smile he sat down under the tree and resumed his leaning. Casca fell asleep while daydreaming. He was awakened by someone gently shaking him. Judging by the sun, he must have been asleep for several hours.

"Casca," said the young Legionnaire. "Wake up."

Casca was instantly alert. It was the new guy. That Syrian Jew, what was his name? Oh yeah, Acheron. "What do you want Acheron?" Casca asked.

"Sergeant Sporus has sent me to fetch you," Acheron said. "He said it was time to dispatch the dog and serve it to him. The dog is in the cage by the cooking hearth."

Casca leaped to his feet, his bad mood had instantly returned. "I will be there shortly," Casca said in a low growl. Acheron stepped back and bowed his head.

"I want no trouble from you, sir," Acheron said. "I'm just following my orders." Acheron turned and started walking up the hill toward the main camp.

Casca let him get several paces ahead before he reluctantly headed toward the camp. He was muttering obscenities under his breath the whole way. As Casca entered the camp, the fire in the cooking hearth was glowing low. The Legion, for the most part had already eaten dinner. A few stragglers remained behind. They wisely kept out of Casca's way. Sergeant Sporus was nowhere around. Probably in his casa behind the walls. Probably waiting on Casca to serve him as if Casca were a slave, and not the legionnaire that he was, Casca thought. Casca approached the serving table and grabbed a piece of meat and a chunk of bread. He placed the meat on the bread and took a bite. Nodding in satisfaction, he headed to the cage. Peering in, he saw the dog, lying on his side, eyes closed. A lamb was licking the dogs head. How peculiar Casca thought.

"What to do with you," Casca said, unlatching the cage, and walking in. The lamb scrambled away. Pytre opened his eyes and slowly got to his feet. The several hours of deep sleep had done Pytre wonders. Pytre approached the man, never breaking eye contact with him.

"You are a tough one," said Casca. Casca held his sandwich in one hand and his sword in the other. "Are you hungry boy?" Casca held out his sandwich. Pytre stopped moving and let out a low snarl.

"And a proud one," Casca chuckled. "You don't really trust or like your capturers." Casca sheathed his sword and sat down by the side of the cage. He broke off a piece of meat and tossed it to the dog. Pytre sniffed the meat; he had not eaten in a couple of days. Casca leaned against the cage wall, and took a big bite out of his sandwich. "It's very good, boy," Casca said with his mouth full of food. Pytre sniffed the meat one more time, and then gobbled it down. The food gave Pytre some much needed nourishment. Pytre looked at the man, and nodded thanks.

Casca roared with laughter. "You are welcome," Casca said. He broke off another piece of meat and threw it to the dog. Pytre ate it, and nodded in thanks again. Casca finished his sandwich, occasionally sharing a piece with the dog. When it was done, Casca sat there thinking. Pytre remained where he was, several feet away.

"Okay," Casca said. "I like you. More importantly, I really hate Sergeant Sporus. Go on boy, get out of here." Casca nodded toward the open cage door.

Pytre got up, and walked to the door. At the door he turned back toward the man, and nodded one time. Then Pytre turned and bolted out the cage heading in the direction he had been traveling when he was struck by the man.

Casca was laughing. "Must be an important mission, you dumb mutt," Casca said. "You are headed toward Golgotha. You really don't want to be there this weekend. We are expecting all kinds of trouble there." Casca reached under his cloak and grabbed his wine skin. It was full. Smiling, Casca consumed its contents, and fell into a blissful sleep.

* * * * * * * *

Casca woke to the sound of Sergeant Sporus screaming. "Casca," Sporus shouted. "You have got to be the stupidest idiot I know. You not only let the dog escape, but three of the pigs are missing too." Casca looked out into the compound, soldiers and animals were running around all Helter Skelter.

Casca started laughing. Sporus' backhand brought Casca to his feet, he was glaring at Sporus. Both men had their hands on the hilt of their sword. "Casca," Sporus said in a low tight voice. "You have crucifixion duty this weekend. Your pass is cancelled."

"Yes Sergeant," Casca said. Casca straightened, and walked out of the cage.

"Acheron," Sporus bellowed. "You had a mission and you failed. You have crucifixion duty also. Take your friend Kleton with you."

"Yes Sergeant," both men said at once.

Sergeant Sporus surveyed the situation. Satisfied that discipline had been restored and justice dispensed, he straightened his cloak and walked out of the cage.

* * * * * * * *

Casca, Acheron, and Kleton reported to the *praetorium*, the temporary residence of their Prefect, Pontius Pilate. All three were freshly shaved and in their cleanest uniform. They were joined by fifteen other legionnaires who were reporting for this dubious duty. Casca was, arguably, the best looking of the group. Although he had a raised red mark on the side of his face from Sporus' back hand, Casca was rugged, but symmetrical. He also was clearly of Roman heritage, and he had a determined fire blazing in his eyes. Most of the legionnaires liked him. However, some hated him, but few didn't have an opinion about him. It was no surprise when the Captain of the Guard chose Casca and his team to perform the escort duty to Golgotha with the celebrity criminal, 'The King of the Jews.'

"Damn it," said Casca. "Let us be extremely careful." Casca was secretly proud. He loved the limelight, and this mission was extremely dangerous. He grabbed a bull whip from the armory.

As they brought the prisoners out, Casca' jaw dropped for a moment. What was going on here Casca thought? There were two murderers; both looked scared, but otherwise okay. Then the 'King of the Jews' came trailing in. He looked unafraid, but exhausted. He had been flogged and tortured. A crown of thorns had been hammered into his head. His simple white garment was stained in blood and sweat.

Casca was amazed and a little alarmed at the majestic way the prisoner carried himself. Using his bull whip in his right had, he pointed at the patibulum, or cross beam of the cross. 'You," Casca commanded. "Pick up your burden, and move out."

Jesus, struggling, grabbed the patibulum and lifted it. It weighed about seventy-five pounds, over half of Jesus' own weight. He hefted it to his shoulders. He was extremely weak due to the loss of blood. Stumbling, he headed down the path as legionnaire Kleton cleared the way. Casca looked on, proud of his men, but somewhat uneasy.

The precession cleared the gate of the *praetorium*. A dog broke through the crowd and ran up to Jesus. The crowd scattered among the growls and barks. It was Pytre.

Jesus dropped the crossbeam, and reached down and hugged Pytre. "My friend," Jesus said. "Our time here is short." Pandemonium broke out all around the place.

Casca, bull whip raised, breaks through the crowd, and surveys the scene. Spotting Pytre he lowers his bull whip to a half mast position, "You," he says. "Why am I not fucking surprised?" He drops his bull whip to his side. Pytre and Jesus both looked at him with determined piercing eyes.

"You," Casca said pointing to a man in the crowd. "Pick up his patibulum and move out." The man complied. Jesus fell in behind the man, limping, weak from blood loss and lack of sleep. Pytre walked by his side. Pytre was also limping. Casca and Acheron brought up the rear. Together the convoy made its slow ascent to Golgotha and a place in history.

* * * * * * *

Pytre lay a few feet from the cross. He was looking up at his master who was nailed to this insidious device. Pytre was whimpering softly and his breathing had become labored. Slowly Pytre closed his eyes. He could feel his master gently caressing him, and whispering words of comfort to him. Pytre opened one eye. His master was still nailed to the cross. Pytre closed the eye and could feel his master's presence again. He kept his eyes closed preferring this reality to the other. Pytre could hear Jesus' voice in his head telling him to sleep, and they would be together soon in the great beyond. Pytre gave a long deep contented sigh, and expired.

CHAPTER ELEVEN

The Meeting Number Three

San Diego, California
10 June 2011

Karen and Curt were having a leisurely brunch at *Rock Hounds* when Curt got the phone call on his cell phone. "Curt, this is Mike," Commander Wayne said. "How long before you can make it back here?"

"About two hours," Curt said.

"Great," said Mike. "You've actually got three. Something big has come up. Bring Samson. We are moving the meeting time up. See you at thirteen hundred." Mike hung up.

Karen reached over and touched Curt's hand. "Problems?" she asked. Curt jumped as she touched him. She was falling in love with him, but he was so non-personal, so self contained. Samson seemed to be the only one he appeared relaxed with.

"Ah, no," Curt said. "It's just another meeting at work. This Pytre case just keeps getting weirder and weirder. I don't like weird. I don't like ghosts, and I especially don't like things from the supernatural world."

"Hey," Karen said. She was getting excited now as she often did when she was with Curt. "Did I ever tell you about when I saw the ghost of my dead grandfather?"

"No," Curt said. He got up and gave Karen a kiss on the cheek. "I got to go." Curt pulled out a fifty dollar bill and laid it on the table, and turned and started to walk away.

Karen flushed with anger. She was also very hurt. "Why don't we let Pytre pick up the tab?" She shouted at his retreating figure.

"What?" Curt asked. He had spun around and advanced to here so fast that it had startled her. "Pytre is here?" Curt asked. He stared at her with deep piercing blue eyes. They were hard, but also a little bit scared. Curt was now scanning the room intently. Karen felt a pang of guilt. This man was so innocent, yet so very dangerous.

"No," Karen said. "I'm sorry. I was trying to be funny. Well, no, I was mad. I wanted you to hear my grandfather ghost story."

Curt's gazed returned to Karen's eyes. "Maybe later," Curt said. "I've got to go to a meeting now." He bent over and kissed her gently on her lips. "I'd love to see you when I get back." Without waiting for an answer, Curt turned around and headed for the door. Samson got up from under the table and walked up to Karen.

"Will you see me again too?" Karen asked, scratching Samson's head. In reply, Samson licked both Karen's arms, and then licked her square across the face. Karen giggled. Samson spun around and took off after Curt.

Curt was almost to the gate when Samson started, so Samson had to put on a renewed burst of speed in his effort. Samson knew that the leader set the pace. It was up to each pack member to keep up with that pace. You either arrived at the fight on time or you were just a punk ass rabbit. Samson could hear in his mind, his master's voice say the words a punk ass rabbit. He had heard them a hundred times in training at the K9 Trident Warrior School. He could not have written them, or described them, but he knew what it meant. After all, they were just communicating. Samson hit the gate three inches before it closed, and pushed through taking stride next to Curt's right heel as they approached Curt's car. Samson was happy. Bullets and bombs were healed and forgotten. The future looked promising.

Curt opened the trunk to his car. Samson leaped in while Curt closed the trunk. Samson did a sweep of the trunk, and then pushed through a secret passage to the back seat where he continued his sweep of the car. Finding everything all clear with no strange scents, Samson pushed the unlock button on the center console. Curt opened the driver's door and got in. It was all done very quickly. The studious observer, at best would have seen a man open his trunk, a dog leap in while the man was not looking, and a similar dog appear to be in the car when the man got in.

Curt started the car while Samson settled in the passenger seat and fastened his dog harness. Curt reached over and scratched the side of Samson's head. "Braafy Samson," Curt said continuing to scratch Samson's head. "I can't be getting blown up again," Curt said. "I don't make enough money to keep buying you all those chickens." Curt laughed. Samson wagged his tail. They had communicated. His master had just told him that he was a good dog and a valued member of the pack. Humans sure did have a lot of different words to say the same thing.

Karen watched from the café. She was falling in love with both of them.

* * * * * * * *

Five minutes from 1300 hours Curt and Samson entered the briefing room. Curt was in his Navy camouflage uniform. Samson was wearing a collar that had his name on it plus an embossed Bronze Star with V device, a Purple Heart, and the Trident K9 Warrior emblem. This was a belated birthday gift from Karen. He was not allowed to wear it out in public, but could proudly wear it when at work. His lead trailed behind him. Curt bent down and unhooked Samson's lead. Curt then sat at his assigned seat. Samson laid down on the floor to the right of Curt's Chair. Curt looked across from him and nodded hello to Fred, his CIA buddy.

Mike, Captain Martinez, and an Army Colonel entered the room. "Attention," Mike said. Everybody, including Samson rose to their feet. Captain Martinez occupied the chairman seat. Mike was to his right, and the Army Colonel was to his left. Captain Martinez surveyed the room. He nodded in satisfaction, and said, "Please take your seats." Everybody, including Samson sat down. From his sit position, Samson's head was now visible above the table.

Captain Martinez, now seated, looked around the room. "Nice collar Samson," he said. Samson, hearing his name nodded. Commander Mike Wayne was grinning in pride.

"Now that we know where to pin the medals," Mike said. "We can award a lot more of them." There was laughter all around the room.

"Fred," Captain Martinez said. "Welcome back. I have you and your most interesting findings near the beginning of this briefing."

Fred nodded and said, "Thank you sir."

"Curt," Captain Martinez said. "Your medical was top line. Are you ready to stop milking the tax payer, and come back on active duty?"

"Yes sir," said Lieutenant Curtis Mays.

"You know," Captain Martinez continued. "Your father and I worked together during Grenada. I was sorry to hear of his passing. He was an excellent man and a credit to the Navy."

"Thank you sir," said Curt.

"Well let's get started," said Captain Martinez. "To my left is Colonel Tim Kolinsky. In light of recent developments, the Army is now joining us on Project Pytre Dawg. Fred? If you would tell us what you discovered in Norfolk, Virginia please."

Fred removed a thumb drive from his tie clip and stuck it into the computer at his station. "Thank you sir," Fred said. "Gentleman," Fred continued as he glanced around the room. "I just returned from Norfolk this morning. Some very interesting developments have occurred. For background, is everybody familiar with the fictional series of books entitled *Casca: The Eternal Mercenary*? It was written by a man named Barry Sadler, a Special Forces operator who served in Vietnam." There were nods of yes around the room except for Curt.

"I'm not familiar with that story," said Curt.

Colonel Kolinsky straightened his glasses, looking incredulously. "He wrote the very popular song, The Ballard of the Green Beret," Kolinsky said. "You know, a hundred men will test today, but only three win the Green Beret. That's why I joined the Army and went Special Forces."

"Sorry sir," Curt said. "I was raised in a Navy family. I remember hearing that song when I was a kid, but I don't know a thing about any eternal mercenaries, and I've never heard of the name Casca before."

It's okay," Fred said raising his hand. "I'll give you the background. Vietnam has been a war torn hot bed of activity since World War Two. Shortly after the French pulled out in the mid fifties, the United States started sending in intelligence operators and advisors. Under the Kennedy Administration, a special operations group popularly known as the Green Berets was formed. They were sent over to Vietnam as advisors in the early sixties. By the mid sixties there was a legend among the Green Berets about this two thousand year old warrior fighting in Vietnam. According to legend this man was at the crucifixion and was cursed by Jesus Christ himself to remain on Earth as a warrior until the second coming. This man would never age, and his wounds, even fatal ones would heal rapidly and on their own accord. A Special Forces medic named Barry Sadler who was serving in Vietnam during this time period, later penned a whole series of books about this man. In the fictional series by Barry Sadler, this man's name was Casca Rufio Longinius. However in book one; Casca is using an alias of Casey Romain, who is now an American soldier. Now, hold on to your seats gentleman." Fred touched his computer and a picture of a white haired old man appeared on the wall.

"This man is Chris Matthews," Fred continued. "He is currently living in Norfolk, Virginia. He was an orderly who worked the Mental Ward at Norfolk General from 1962 until 1984. He was the orderly who escorted our Pytre Dawg murdering John Doe when he was attacked and killed by wild dogs. I had the pleasure of talking to this elderly gentleman for several hours. Chris is a very sharp man. He also had the pleasure of talking to, and getting to know our John Doe. It seems that our John Doe's real name is Casey Alfred Romain." Curt gasped.

"Hang in there Curt," Fred said. He touched some more buttons on his computer, and the John Doe autopsy photo appeared. Then an old Army enlistment photo appeared, followed by photocopies of Military Records and Dental Records."

"This is Casey Alfred Romain," Fred said. "He was an early baby boomer, being born on 18 December 1944. He enlisted in the Army on his eighteenth birthday in 1962. He immediately joined the newly formed Special Forces. He obtained the rank of Staff Sergeant, and did two tours of duty in Vietnam. Both tours were with the Special Forces. No direct connect that we can find yet, but it is highly probable that his path could have crossed with Barry Sadler's path. He was at Walter Reed Hospital in early 1968 having a mental evaluation. Most likely suffering from what we now call PTSD. At the time, the closest thing they had was called Battle Fatigue. It was associated with being a coward that cracked in battle. This was definitely not Romain's case. In fact he was just the opposite. He became a risk taker. It was not an easy diagnosis at the time. Before they could make a determination he had murdered his doctor, and three MPs. He then vanished off the face of the Earth. Three months later, John Doe appears at Norfolk General Hospital. Dental Records are sketchy, but several points make it highly probable that John Doe was Casey Romain. Fingerprints are not conclusive, but a partial off the Norfolk General Dental Records make it highly probable that Romain handled John Doe's Dental Records. Gentleman, I am almost one hundred percent certain that John Doe was Staff Sergeant Casey Alfred Romain." The room was a buzz as everybody examined the slides on the wall.

"So," Curt said. "Romain PTSDs out, slips through the crack, and becomes the John Doe that murders Pytre. That puts us back with the Pytre twin as our number one theory. The Romain story is fascinating, but I don't see how it helps us catch Pytre, or why the Army is now involved."

"Which brings me to part two of my briefing," Fred said. The Orderly Chris Mathews Interviews." Everybody sat back down. "Chris," Fred continued. "Told me that Romain had been on the ward about a month before he was allowed in contact, or even knew of the existence of Pytre. Chris and Romain would take smoke breaks together in Romain's room. Romain confessed his real name to Chris, and told him horrific stories about Vietnam. He told him about meeting and fighting with this mercenary over in Vietnam who could not die. He would get horrible wounds, and would heal in a matter of days. Romain told Chris that he and this mercenary became friends. He learned that the man's name was Casca, and that he was two thousand years old. Casca was the one in charge at the crucifixion of Jesus Christ. Christ had made him immortal. Romain also said Casca would tell stories about this dog that was at the crucifixion, and how he had first met that dog earlier that day. Casca told Romain that it was Jesus' dog, and the dog and Jesus died on the same day."

"Now," Fred said, pausing for dramatic affect. "Chris said he did not know about Pytre or Pytre's story. Pytre was in the children's section of the ward, and Chris never went there. According to Chris, Romain never met Pytre until the day that he killed him, when they were left alone together in the main lobby, while waiting for separate medical appointments. After the murder, Chris helped escort Romain. Romain told him that Pytre had said he was the reincarnated dog of Jesus, that he was Son of Dog. Romain said that the devil made him kill Pytre. Romain said that Pytre was going to do good things for the canine world, and would have to be stopped so humans would not be diminished." Fred stopped and spread his hands. "That's it for me for right now," he said.

The room whirled in pandemonium again. Captain Martinez raised his hand for silence. "Colonel Kolinsky started his career by enlisting in the Army Special Forces at the tail end of the Vietnam War. He later received his Medical Doctor's Degree and became an Army Doctor. He currently works at Walter Reed. Go ahead Tim, give us the Army perspective.

"Thank you Dustin," said Colonel Kolinsky rising from his chair. Kolinsky tapped some commands on the keyboard at his station. More documents appeared on the wall. These had green boarders which made them distinguishable from Fred's slides which remained on the wall. "These are the classified psychological reports on Staff Sergeant Casey A. Romain. I have downloaded these to your stations. You may read them at your leisure. Just remember they're top secret, compartment Dawg classification, and treat them accordingly. The important thing to note here is that Romain was spouting his Casca and his Jesus dog rhetoric long before he could have come into contact with Pytre Dawg, the murdered child. It has occurred to us in Army Intelligence that there may be a conspiracy, or a secret sect, or secret religion, which could have come out of Vietnam during the war. Maybe even long before that. This also means our unholy alliance theory has expanded from al-Qaeda and the IRA, to now include a group of disgruntled Vietnam vets." Colonel Kolinsky sat down.

"Thank you Tim," said Captain Martinez. "Before I give out assignments, Fred, you skipped the part about the dogs."

"Oh yeah," said Fred. "The Orderly Chris Mathews disagrees with the verdict that Romain was killed by a pack of wild dogs."

"Thank God," said Curt. "That part bothered me. I mean a pack of wild dogs attack and kill the man who murdered the Son of Dog." Curt made little quotation marks in the air with his hands. "I mean, come on."

"According to Chris," Fred said while looking at Curt and giving his friend a sad smile. "The dogs all had collars, were well feed, and appeared way to healthy to be wild dogs." Curt sat back hard, like he had been punched.

"Thanks Fred," said Captain Martinez. "I'm sending you to Belgium to check out Smithy's old operation. Curt you and Samson are going to Norfolk to check out the hospital, the old carnival site, the place were Romain was killed, and to talk to Chris Mathews. Take Samson with you everywhere. Let me know of any reactions, or lack of reactions from Samson wherever you go. You are taking a C5 Galaxy out of here to Langley. Your flight leaves in an hour. Mike, you are coming with me and Colonel Kolinsky to Washington. I'll brief you on the plane. We've got to leave now. Everybody else stand by at the ready. You are now at cycle green. I repeat, you are now at cycle green. Dismissed."

Everybody leaped to their feet. Captain Martinez, Colonel Kolinsky, and Commander Mike Wayne left the briefing room. Fred was typing stuff into his terminal. The tie clip thumb drive was still attached.

"Come on Samson," Curt said. "We got a plane to catch." Curt got up and started to head toward his car to grab his and Samson's ready bags. Samson trailed behind at his heal position.

CHAPTER TWELVE

Carnival Freaks

Ocean View, Virginia
2 June 1956

Ethel Dawg, better known as The Amazing Dog Girl, waddled into the manager's trailer. She was due at any time now. Her husband, John Dawg, also know as Dog Man, closely followed her in. He held her elbow with his hand giving her support and balance.

"My water just broke," Ethel said.

The manager, a dapper young fellow, spun around from his desk. "Oh my God, oh my God, oh my God," he panted. "Just stay calm. Amber! Get the mid wife. We are about to have a puppy."

Amber, the manager's wife ran to Madame Mystic's trailer. The Freak Show had twelve trailers, parked in a circle around the lot located behind the amusement park. This is where they lived and hung out when they were not performing at the amusement park. Madame Mystic was just opposite of the office, or manager's trailer. The manager's trailer was the largest. That was why it was used for meetings, group meals, surgeries, child birthing, and things like that. Madame Mystic, born Jane Morris, was a clairvoyant. That was not much of a freak by the day's standard, but she was also the doctor, veterinarian, midwife, handy-man, and counselor. The fact that she also brought in her fair share of the money telling fortunes made her an extremely valuable member of the troupe.

"Jane," Amber yelled as she entered the trailer. "It's Ethel, her water just broke." Madame Mystic, who was sitting at her table studying about seven open books, looked up and sighed.

"How far are the contractions?" Madame Mystic asked, moving her reading glasses to the top of her head. "And, has the head crowned?"

Amber looked at her and shrugged. "I don't know," Amber said. "Chris just told me to get you."

"Never, ever," said Madame Mystic. "Leave matters of child birth up to men. I will be there shortly." Madame Mystic put her glasses back over her eyes and started studying again.

"Thank you," said Amber. She curtsied and hurried out of the trailer. Running, she returned to the manager's trailer. The manager was standing at the door rubbing his hands.

"Well," he asked.

"She is on her way," Amber said. "I am to take care of things until she gets here."

The manager stepped aside and let her in. The manager, born Chris Anderson, was also the owner of the Freak Show, but having worked both sides of the law, he liked to keep that fact secret. It gave him a buffer, he was fond of saying. He could always go to get the owner, and then return with the information, the money, a gun, or not return at all. It worked for him, and if it wasn't broken, he didn't fix it. His traveling Freak Show had been camped out at Ocean View for about six months now. This was mostly because of the Dawgs, but also the rent was cheap and the draw was good. They were mobile, but it still took a couple of days to move out. However, this Navy town was a good gig. The manager liked it here. His pack was going to increase by at least one tonight. I mean you never could tell how many babies when it came to the Dawgs.

The Dawgs were a star attraction. They were tied for first on dollar intake with the Amazing Bearded Lady, a hermaphrodite, with large mammary and both male and female reproductive organs. It was amazing how many men would pay a dollar to stare at large breast, and a set of reproduction organs, all in the name of science. But the Dawgs had class that touched at the average American's heart strings. They were a dog pack, with male and bitch, four real off spring, twenty real dogs who played the part as off spring. All hairy, and all well trained at being the American dog pack. They were the heart warming bunch that had overcome tragedy by working together as a loving family.

However, the manager realized that the real world was a dangerous place. He realized that people loved the perfect family, but they also resented it. Especially if they had a harder time then the perfect family did, but the afflicted family still were happier because of each other. This would always lead to violence, and because of that the manager was always very cautious.

Madame Mystic entered the trailer. "Where is Amber," she said.

"In here Jane," Amber said. "Ten centimeters, and the head is crowning."

Madame Mystic and the manager's wife joined the struggling Amazing Dog Girl as she gave birth to the puppy. The manager alerted the camp, and security was formed. All twelve trailers were on alert.

Dusk was falling, and a thunderstorm was moving their way from out over the Atlantic Ocean. It was about ten miles out, and you could hear the rumbling thunder and see the lightning flashes in the distance. The sky grew dark from the clouds at the exact same time that it grew dark from the nightfall. The manager hugged himself and gave a shiver. He had to urinate very badly.

Sticking his head in the door of the now birthing room, the manager said, "Jane, I'm going to go pee on the tree."

The radio was playing in the back ground. Over all the noise Madame Mystic could hear the radio announcer say, "And now, from Romania, Pytre singing *Nearer My God To Thee.*" The music began to play, and a male soprano voice began to sing. Just then a lightning bolt struck about half a mile away. It caused the power to black out for a minute. Due to the angle of the windows, it became bright as daylight in half the trailer, and remained dark in the other half. Madame Mystic looked up from between the legs of The Amazing Dog Girl, and saw, spotlighted on the wall, the crucifix and on the shelf below it, a clay statue of a dog. Suddenly she knew.

"Ahhhhh," Ethel said. She gave one hard push.

"Oh my God," squealed Amber! "Here comes the puppy."

"Come Pytre," said Madame Mystic. Pytre slipped from the womb. The afterbirth came out seconds later. Madame Mystic took the sterile knife out of her boot and cut the umbilical chord. She grabbed a single thread of twine from her wrist and tied off the end.

Everybody gathered around the tiny newborn. He looked very hairy. Madame Mystic took a towel and started cleaning him off. Pytre began to cry.

"Why did you call him Pytre?" Ethel asked. She was struggling to sit up. Madame Mystic took the newborn up to Ethel's waiting arms. She continued to wipe him off with the towel. As she cleaned him, his fur came off on the towel. The skin below was of various colors. Pytre stopped crying and began to coo in his mother's arms. The Amazing Dog Girl began licking her new pup clean. Pytre continued cooing. It appeared that he was going to be completely hairless. But his skin, it was very weird looking, almost like hair; just that it was his skin. Like a costume artist appeared to make him up as a dog using stains on the skin. Ethel looked at Madame Mystic quizzically. "Why did you call him Pytre?" She asked again.

"Well," said Madame Mystic. "Don't ask me how I know, but I just do." She took a deep sigh, and then continued. "That is his name. He is the reincarnated dog who belonged to Jesus Christ himself. He was sent to this world now to do great things for dogs and their relationships with humans."

The manager came busting in. You could hear all the dogs in the background barking and carrying on like crazy. "Its gone crazy out there," the manager said. "The dogs all sense the new addition. Is it just one?"

Madame Mystic nodded in the affirmative. She went over to Ethel who had finished cleaning the baby, and gently started stroking Pytre's face. "His name is Pytre," Madame Mystic said. "I had a vision. He is the reincarnated dog who belonged to Jesus Christ. He was sent to us to perform a great mission, and help in the bonding between man and dog."

The manager looked at them for a while, and then nodded. "Better do this one legal," he said. "Take Pytre to a doctor in the real world tomorrow."

All eyes turned to Pytre, who was cradled in his momma's arms and wrapped in the towel that had been used to clean him. He was wiggling in a jerky newborn fashion, a huge smile on his face. He was continuing to make cooing sounds as Madame Mystic stroked the side of his face. All of a sudden, Pytre stopped cooing. He took a deep inhalation, and said, "Woof."

Amber gasped and covered her mouth with her hand. Tears were rolling down her cheek. Ethel and Madame Mystic were openly weeping. John Dawg had tears running down his cheek as he knelt down by the bed and clutched his wife and new son.

"I'd better make sure everything is all secure in the camp," said the manager. He turned before they could see he had tears on his face. Must be something in his eye he thought. Then his thoughts drifted to what a wonderful and miraculous event had just happened. Then he steeled his thoughts to secure the camp. It occurred to him that life for the troupe had probably just gotten harder.

* * * * * * * *

As morning broke on Sunday, 3 June 1956, the Dawg family, human and canine was sitting on the beach watching the sun burst out of the Atlantic Ocean. It was the most spectacular sunrise any of them had ever seen. The storm of the night before caused a kaleidoscope of colors in the morning sky. Ethel sat cuddling her newborn son. It started with the canines; they began a joyous howling at the rising sun. Then the human Dawgs joined in. Then the whole freak show started howling. Dogs could be heard howling all up and down the beach. The sound traveled westward with the rising sun. Pytre was back. This time he was human.

CHAPTER THIRTEEN

Meeting of the Witnesses

Norfolk, Virginia
12 June 2011

The C5 Galaxy taxied to a stop at the end of the runway at Langley Air Force Base, Virginia. Curt and Samson got up and stretched. Curt grabbed their two bags.

"The two supercargo that are debarking here will deplane on the runway," the pilot said over the intercom. "You have about two minutes."

An Air Force Master Sergeant came up to Curt and saluted, "Follow me Captain," The Master Sergeant said. Then he glanced back at Curt's navy uniform. "I mean Lieutenant," he said. "Sorry sir. We don't get many of your kind here. I mean you guys do have your own airplanes."

"Its okay Chief," Curt said with a chuckle. "I mean Master Sergeant. Every now and then we just like to fly in luxury."

The Master Sergeant was grinning now and shook his head. He glanced down at Samson. "Please tell me sir," the Master Sergeant said. "That your dog doesn't out rank me."

"Not yet," said Curt. "But he is on the fast track. He will probably out rank me soon." The Master Sergeant noticed Samson's collar with the Bronze Star with V device for valor, the Purple Heart, and the Seal Team emblem. He nodded with respect, turned, and escorted the two seals to the door. He opened the door and they all watched as a motorized stair case drove toward the plane. A Navy sedan was following it. They watched in silence as the stair case docked.

"Gentlemen," said the Air Force Master Sergeant. He saluted them both. "Good luck on your mission. May you be successful and return to your homes safely." Curt returned the salute and then shook the Master Sergeant's hand. Curt and Samson headed down the stairs to the awaiting sedan. Both passenger doors were open. A young Navy Ensign was standing by the front passenger door. As Curt and Samson approached, the Navy Ensign snapped to attention.

"Good morning sir," said the ensign. He rendered a salute. "I am Ensign Rocky Austin. I will be your driver and guide while you are here. I have been stationed here a little over a year, but I grew up in this area. I know, I know, sir, a Navy oversight. However, that means I do know my way around this area."

Samson leaped in the back seat. Curt shut Samson's door and then climbed in the front seat. Ensign Austin shut Curt's door and hurried over to the driver's side. He got in and started the car. As the sedan headed for the side gate of the runway, Curt noticed the C5 Galaxy he had been on taxi back down the runway and take off. It was now headed to Germany, with some experimental vehicles in its belly. Curt and Samson had piggybacked off the flight. One thing was obvious to Curt and that was that some very important people were now interested in this case.

At the gate, the guard checked their credentials. He made a phone call, and then unlocked the gate and lowered the barrier. Ensign Austin drove the sedan onto the streets of the base.

"Lieutenant Mays," said Ensign Austin. "I've been briefed on part of your mission. I'm to take you to the Amusement Park, the Hospital, and to Chris Matthew's apartment in Colonial Place. I have also been instructed to take you where ever you need to go. I've got a route planned that takes us to the Amusement Park first. What are your instructions, sir?"

"That's fine," said Curt. "We will hit the Amusement Park first, and then play it by ear. We will follow the leads. Did you say your name was Rocky? Rocky Austin?"

"Yes sir," said Rocky. "I grew up in Norfolk. My dad use to tell me stories about the Ocean View Amusement Park. He used to love that place when he was a kid. He went Navy also, but he was enlisted. He retired as a Master Chief. He wanted me to go officer. I went to Old Dominion University for a year, and then I transferred over to the Navel Academy."

"Tell me about Ocean View," Curt said. "Did you every go there as a kid?"

"No sir," said Rocky. "I wasn't born yet when they shut her down. That would have been Labor Day of 1978. My dad grew up in Norfolk, but he never got stationed here until 1985. I wasn't born until 1988. My dad has stayed on at Norfolk ever since. He retired in 1990. He lives in Virginia Beach now though." Rocky turned the sedan on to Granby Street and headed toward the ocean.

"I have been there several times with my dad when I was a kid, even though it was after it was closed," Rocky said. "They told me you would be looking for the place where the old Carnival Freaks used to live. That burnt down in 1958. It's just beach front now, but I can show you exactly where it used to be. My dad went there as a kid. He used to tell me stories of the Dog Family. They were like human dogs. There was a dad and a mom, and about twenty some dog children. They all wore human clothes, but they looked like dogs. My dad used to tell me that he suspected some of them really were just dogs. They would do this act of sitting down at the dinner table, saying the blessing, eating their dinner, then they would all watch TV until time to tuck them into bed. You know, like it was a real human family. I sure wish I could have seen it." Curt just nodded.

Rocky parked the car in a beach front parking space. "Here we are sir," he said. Curt slipped Samson's lead on him. Since they were all in uniform, Samson got to continue to wear his fancy collar. They all started walking toward the beach. Samson was wagging his tail and seemed very excited.

"This part up here was the amusement park," Rocky said. "At one time it boasted *The Rocket,* a humongous roller coaster that my dad said you could probably see from space. I doubt if it were that big, but still it must have been rather impressive. Over there, where that shopping plaza is, used to be the arcades, it was kind of like a big building filled with carnival games and souvenir shops. Down this beach line, between the roller coaster and the ocean were the rides and shows. That's where the Dog Family would have been set up." They walked down the beach in silence for a while. Samson, on his lead, sniffed and investigated everything.

As they got to a little jetty, Samson alerted, then sat down hard, and released a tremendous howl. It wasn't an anguished howl, but more like a call of the wild type howl. Curt dropped down beside Samson and placed his hand on Samson's side. He looked up at Rocky. Samson became quiet.

"Well," said Curt. "I guess this is the place where the dog show was."

"No sir," said Rocky. "That place we just walked through was where all the shows were set up. Well, according to my dad, anyway." Rocky scratched the side of his head. "I think this is where the Carnival Freaks lived and hung out on their off time. My dad said they used to call this place Freakville. It was only here a couple of years. It burnt down in 1958." They stayed there a few more minutes. Samson seemed content.

"I think that's all we can do here for now," Curt said. "What's next?"

"Well sir," Rocky said. "The Hospital is a few miles down that way, off of Colley Avenue in the downtown district. Then we could circle back to do the interview with Chris Mathews. He is expecting us late this afternoon. He lives in Colonial Place in an apartment on Pennsylvania Avenue. Then, no matter how late you stay, we are only a few blocks from my house on Mayflower. I've got a guest bedroom you could use. The Navel Base is about twenty miles away. We also have the Samson issue with many of the hotels downtown." He looked at Curt and shrugged.

Curt smiled, "Sounds like a real good plan Ensign Austin," Curt said. "Let's rock and roll." They all three headed back to the car.

The path had been cleared to take Samson with them to the ninth floor. He had to remain on his leash and under the control of somebody at all times. The ninth floor was now a rehab center for seriously injured people that had to learn how to take care of themselves again. Usually this meant some type of spinal or brain accident, but it also included a few stroke victims.

As the elevator doors opened on the ninth floor, Samson began wagging his tail very energetically. There was a very old lady in a wheel chair sitting in the lobby facing the elevators. When she saw Samson she gave a half smile with the left side of her mouth and face, while the right side remained frozen. She waved her left hand and wrist.

"Samson," she said in a raspy slurred voice. Curt gave a start, and then he remembered that Samson had his name on his collar. Samson tugged on the lease until Curt gave a quick warning tug. When they walked by her the lady reached over and touched Samson. Samson began licking her hand as she scratched the side of his head.

"Ms. Morris," said an orderly, all dressed in white except for his black tennis shoes. "You know better than to play with a strange dog. I'm going to have to take you back to your room." He was moving briskly toward her.

"It's okay," said Curt. "He has got a secondary as a companion dog."

"It is not okay," said the orderly. "She is stroked out, and doesn't have any awareness of her surroundings. Probably doesn't even know where she is. She can't be grabbing at wild animals."

"She is aware enough," said Curt stiffly. "To read this wild animal's dog collar from a hundred feet away." The orderly reached the wheelchair and roughly took hold of it. The old lady looked up from scratching Samson.

"Samson's friend," the old lady said in that slurred speech. "You will probably want to talk to me, but first you must talk to the manager." She gave Curt a half smile, and Samson one last pat. The orderly pushed her away.

A middle aged man in a suit came rushing up. "Lieutenant Mays and Ensign Austin I presume," he said extending his hand to Curt. "I'm Murray Carlson. I'm an administrator around here. I'm here to escort you around the hospital." Curt shook his hand. He had calmed down from his encounter with the orderly. "This must be Samson," Carlson said. "I have been briefed on his special abilities, but I ask that he stay with you the whole time." Curt nodded in the affirmative.

The foursome toured the ninth floor. Samson sniffed and investigated everything. Samson showed no more interest in anything. Not even at the murder location. Only when they were headed back out did Samson alert again. It was when they passed a private room. The name plate said Jane Morris. Samson started wagging his tail and pulled once on his lead. Curt looked in and saw that it was the old lady in the wheel chair.

"Mr. Carlson," Curt said pausing in front of the room. "What's the story on this one? Samson has taken a fancy to her."

"Not much to tell," said Carlson. "Her name is Jane Morris. She was brought in here about six months ago by her grandniece. She had a stroke and was paralyzed. She is actually making a good recovery. I mean she is ninety-four years old. She can now move part of her left side and has some, although limited speech abilities. Her grandniece is a delightful person who faithfully visits her every Sunday."

Curt nodded. He could not see how this fit in with the case, but he trusted Samson. This lady was important somehow.

"Well she apparently likes dogs," Curt said. "That makes her a-okay in my book." They all chuckled. The three Navy personnel made their farewells at the elevator and departed.

When they were all three in the sedan, Rocky looked at his watch. "It is fifteen thirty-five sir," he said. "Are you ready to go see Mr. Chris Matthews?"

"Let's Rock," said Curt. Rocky put the car in gear and moved out. They rode down Colley until they got to Thirty-Eighth Street, made a right and headed south. When they got to Newport Avenue they made a left. Eight blocks later they were at the corner of Newport and Pennsylvania Avenue. Rocky made a right and parked on the corner in front of a quadraplex apartment building.

"He's on the second floor," Rocky said. "On the left, it is apartment number four." They all got out and entered the building. Curt didn't bother to put Samson on a leash. Curt knocked on the door. After a few moments the door opened. A bright eyed, white haired old man answered the door.

"It's the United States Navy," said Chris. "You must be Lieutenant Curt Mays. Fred told me to expect you." Chris shook Curt's hand. "And this must be Ensign Rocky Austin. We talked on the phone last night. Good to meet you in person." Chris shook Rocky's hand. Then Chris dropped to his knees.

"This is definitely Samson," Chris said. He ruffled Samson's head and ears. Samson's tail was wagging in overdrive.

"Samson, please," Curt said. "Show some professionalism."

"It's okay," said Chris standing up. "We are all Navy here. Where are my manners, please come in." Curt looked perplexed.

"Mr. Matthews," said Curt, sitting down on the couch in the main room of the efficiency.

"Please," Chris said. "Call me Chris."

"Chris," said Curt. "I'm confused here. You said you were in the Navy. Now I have done a complete background check on you. You were born Christopher James Matthews on 10 October 1923. Then there is no record of you until you become an orderly at Norfolk General in 1962. You were thirty-eight then. No school records and we did keep records back in those days. You made it through World War Two and the Korean Conflict without a trace. Help me out here."

"Well," said Chris. He sighed. Samson had scrunched over toward the easy chair he was sitting in, and Chris started absent mindedly scratching Samson's head. "I wasn't always Chris Matthews."

"So the birth certificate is a fake," Curt said. He had a copy of it pulled up on his laptop.

"No," said Chris. "I was born Chris Mathews. That is my real birth certificate you are looking at. That is my real baby footprint on the certificate. My widowed mother remarried a man named Jack Anderson when I was about four. I was adopted and issued a new adoption birth certificate in 1928. I was then officially Christopher James Anderson. I attended school here in Norfolk under that name. I enlisted in the Navy in early 1942 under that name. I served on the USS Indianapolis under that name. I was honorable discharged from said Navy under that name, and I owned my own business up until 28 February 1958 under that name."

Curt typed in the new information on his laptop through a secure link, and watched as all the new data popped up on his screen. They sat in silence as Curt ran through all the Anderson documents.

"An impressive record Petty Officer Anderson," said Curt. "Thank you for your service. Why didn't you remain Anderson?"

"Some legal problems," said Chris. "There is no statute of limitations for murder Lieutenant Mays. While you have your computer out, check your sources for this. I got a Doing Business As permit with a vending license in 1946. I called my operation the Carnival Freaks."

The preverbal light bulb went off in Curt's brain like a nuclear bomb. "Oh my God," Curt said. "You knew Pytre. You knew Pytre from the time he was born."

Chris nodded. "In fact," he continued. "I was there when he was born. I was also there when his parents and family got murdered." A tear rolled down Chris's cheek. Samson put his head in Chris's lap. Curt and Rocky remained raptly silent.

"It was the twenty-eighth of February 1958," Chris said. "Pytre was about a year and a half old. I was at the Amusement Park main office negotiating an extended lease. They called themselves the Nazi Killers. They were a band of eight men who had fought against the Nazis in World War Two, but they acted more like Nazis then the people they were protesting against."

"It's funny," Chris continued. "How terror organizations give themselves such lofty names, like the freedom fighters, or liberation armies, or peacekeepers. Never has a school been blown up by a group that more aptly called themselves, The Army of Assholes That Go Around Hurting People." Curt laughed in spite of himself.

"Anyway," said Chris. "These Nazi Killer guys grabbed Amber, my wife, she was a real looker, and tried to have their way with her. She was also a fighter, and they had their hands full. She was screaming, kicking, scratching, and raising hell with them. So they beat her very badly, even broke her jaw and two of her ribs. Well Ethel, that's Pytre's mom, we called her the Amazing Dog Girl, hears the commotion and takes off like an attack dog. She leaps on the back of one of the attackers. That really seemed to set them off. They start screaming about all the fucking freaks and started hitting Ethel with chains. Amber escapes and runs to the Dawg trailer. She gets John, which was Pytre's dad, and lets him know what's going on. So John grabs Pytre and hands him to Amber who is hurt pretty bad. Then John grabs a kitchen knife, not much of a weapon, and heads out to save his wife. Amber is very weak now and is fading fast. She makes it a couple of trailers over to Jane's place. Jane was our jack of all trades gal, she could do anything, we called her Madame Mystic. Amber hands the baby to Jane and tells her to go get the manager, which was me, and tell me that we are under attack. Then Amber passed out. I don't know what happened after that because Amber was the one who told me the story."

Chris paused for a moment, and then started weeping. Curt and Rocky sat sad eyed and silent. Samson let out a little moan. Chris took a deep sigh.

"Well," Chris continued. "It took Madame Mystic a while to find me. By the time I got there our trailer camp had been burnt down. All the Dawgs, human and canine were dead. Most of our troupe was dead. I found

Amber unconscious next to Madame Mystic's trailer. All that was left of us was Amber, who was very badly hurt, Jane, Pytre, and myself. We slowly nursed Amber back to health. She told us the whole story. She also identified the attackers. They didn't try to hide very well. We didn't go to the police, what for, we were just a bunch of carnival freaks. I tracked down all eight assailants and killed them, and not very pleasantly either."

Curt sucked in his breath. "Maybe you shouldn't tell us that part," he whispered. Rocky was nodding in the affirmative.

"Lordy," Chris chuckled. "That's exactly what Fred said." Curt became wild eyed.

Rocky looked quizzically at Curt.

"That son of a bitch," Curt said. "You told Fred this story. He didn't even give me a heads up. That rat bastard."

"Fred of the CIA," Chris said mockingly. "I saw his CIA badge. No last name, no middle name. He is just Fred of the CIA. We all have secrets, but I bet Fred has some that would make all our hair stand up." They all laughed at that. Even Samson was enjoying the reduction in tension. They were communicating.

Chris told the story about Pytre's birth, to include the thunder storm and Madame Mystic's claim that Pytre was the Son of Dog. It was after midnight when they concluded, and they all agreed to meet back in the morning.

* * * * * * * *

"Chris," Curt said the next morning. "I want to hear all about Pytre, but first we need to jump ahead to your orderly days at Norfolk General, and the John Doe patient that murdered Pytre. I believe he was a PTSD Vietnam veteran who was Casey Romain." All four of the team, including Samson, were currently chowing down on seafood breakfast tacos that Rocky had picked up from *Lewis's*, the seafood deli around the creek from where he lived. The atmosphere was relaxed. Curt was actually enjoying the mysteries this case provided.

"First, let's clear the air sir; Curt." Chris said, he looked down at the floor as he said it. He paused, took a deep breath, and sighed. "Fred told me about Iraq. I would like to hear your version. I know this will be difficult."

"Aggghhhh," Curt moaned. He was at the threshold. Samson reached over and licked his hand. Curt gathered strength. "Okay," Curt said. "I am starting to accept that there are things in this world that are …. Bizarre! I am not a religious person. I do not believe in the supernatural. There is the real world, and then there is make believe. Make believe is not real. It can never be real." Curt paused, and rubbed his forehead.

"It was in 2006," Curt continued. "I was in Iraq. The operation had gone sour. Fred had taken a few rounds from an AK-47. One of them was in his chest and was causing him some serious problems. We had no communications. Our radio and cell phones had been destroyed. I desperately needed to get some help. I'm carrying Fred. Just then my father appears down the block. He is wearing his dress uniform. He points to a door and motions me to come here. The big problem here is that my father had died two years before. I look down at Fred and he shakes his head yes. I follow my father into the building where he points out a fully functioning radio. However, I don't have a CEOI. I don't know the frequencies, call signs, or any of the codes. My dad tells me to put the radio on 3030, and say Alpha six niner this is Charlie four two. X-ray Romeo, Red Horse down, meet me at tree top south. Fred is shaking his head absolutely yes. I send the message. My dad then tells me to go down the street to the town square. I haul Fred down there, and five minutes later a dust off helicopter picks us up. They say they got my radio call. I looked it up in the CEOI when I got back to the base. The message was correct. I never told anybody about seeing my dad. Fred and I never even discussed it. Is his story similar?"

"Yes," said Chris. "It is the same story, but from different perspectives. Fred is a remarkable person. Thank you for sharing." The room was silent for a while. Everyone was lost in their own thoughts. Except for Samson, who was growling at his own tail.

"I believe you were asking about Casey Romain," Chris said, breaking the silence and the mood. "I had been working at Norfolk General for about six years when he was brought in. I did not know that Pytre was there. The ninth floor was a Pysch ward then, and Pytre was a minor. There were a lot of privacy issues. Besides, I thought he was still with Jane, or Madame Mystic. We didn't keep in touch that much any more. Amber had died shortly after my last murder of the Dawg killers. I think she died of a broken heart. She was never the same after that night. Jane took care of Pytre, and I assumed my new identity. Casey was brought in as a John Doe. He was in my section of the ward. A real personable guy and we used to play checkers and smoke cigarettes in the lobby. He told me his real name and why he had to keep low. He also told me about this man he had met in Vietnam, a two thousand year old warrior who could not die. A man called Casca. Casca was a mercenary working with Romain's team. They had raided a village suspected of being ARVN controlled. Casca took a round to the face, would have killed any man. Casca did not die. Romain dragged him out. As Casca was recuperating he told Romain about this dog. He said he had slashed the dog across the face and his sergeant had hung him pretty good, but the dog was a real fighter. He had fallen for the dog and helped him escape. Later the dog shows up at the crucifixion. It seems that the dog and Jesus are good friends." Chris stops for a moment. He becomes very emotional and buries his face in his hands.

"I think I might have started what happened next," Chris said. "What gets me through is my trust in Pytre." Chris broke down again.

"You see, I told Romain that the dogs name was Pytre and that he was reincarnated as a human now," Chris continued. "The next day I find out Pytre is on the ward, only because he had been murdered. I was going to take Romain out, but Pytre appeared to me that night. He wasn't a vision or a dream, he was there in person. He was all happy and like, hey, it's the manager. He said it was time for him to shed his mortal body. That in dog years he was eighty-four, and he already knew what it felt like to feel cold or hot, hungry, scared, and hurt. Now he had to move a little more quickly. I dropped my plans for revenge, but the next day he was taken out by a pack of dogs. Not wild dogs, but a special assembled group of nearby dogs tasked for the mission." Chris paused again. He took a deep breath and let it out as a sigh.

All of a sudden, Samson let out a deep mournful howl and then he started crying. All three men rushed to his aide. After a few moments, Samson allowed himself to be comforted. Then he licked each man in turn. They all settled back down on the two couches. Everyone was visibly disturbed. Curt nodded for Chris to continue.

"Of course," Chris said. "I wondered what had happened to Jane. I mean, Madame Mystic was very responsible, and she was supposed to have been taking care of Pytre. Something must have happened to her. I finally found her, she was a Jane Doe coma patient in a hospital in Richmond, Virginia. When she recovered, I found out she had been brutally assaulted. She had lost the will to live. She almost bought it, in the preverbal way. One day I came to visit her and she said that Pytre had come to visit her. She was all excited. She was full of a renewed energy. Then her niece got killed. Her niece was a single mom with a little girl. Jane said that she had to take care of her grandniece. I always wondered what happened to them. She would have been ninety-four now." Chris paused again.

Curt shot up like a bolt. It was the number that sparked him. "Shit," Chris screamed! Rocky got it also. They both looked at Chris.

"Chris," Curt said. "Tell me Jane's last name." Both Rocky and Curt were staring at him. Samson was looking very sad.

"It was Morris," Chris said.

"The old lady at the hospital" Curt said. "She is Madame Mystic." Curt pulled out his cell phone and called Murray Carlson, the administrator at Norfolk General.

"Mr. Carlson," Curt said. "Lieutenant Mays here. I need to come back to the hospital to talk to one of your patients. Her name is Jane Morris."

There was a pause on the other end. Curt could hear a women crying in the back ground. "Ahh, Lieutenant Mays," Carlson said. "I'm sorry, but Ms. Morris just past away a few minutes ago." The weeping in the background escalated.

"Damn it," Curt said. "I want a full autopsy on her."

"Well Lieutenant," Carlson said. "She was ninety-four."

"I don't give a damn,' Curt said. "I want a full autopsy on her." He nodded toward Rocky who pulled out his cell phone and made some calls ensuring this request would be honored.

"Lieutenant Mays," said Carlson over the phone. "Faith Ann, her grandniece would like to talk to you." There was sobbing in the back ground that became clearer as she approached the phone.

"Hello," Faith Ann said, sobbing. "I'm supposed to tell a person something. May I ask who you are?"

"I'm Curt," said Curt over the phone. "I talked to your great aunt yesterday at the hospital."

"No," she said. "You're not the one."

"I am Lieutenant Curtis Alfred Mays, deputy commander of Seal Team three," said Curt. "Your great aunt wanted to talk to me yesterday."

"No," said Faith Ann absently. "I'm only supposed to tell it to a certain person."

Curt's head reeled. "She said I would want to talk to her," Curt said. "She said I had to talk to the manager first. I get it now. She knew Samson. She said I was Samson's friend."

"Are you?" Faith Ann asked. "Are you Samson's friend?"

"Yes," said Curt. "I am Samson's friend."

"Then you are the one I'm supposed to tell," said Faith Ann. "I'm supposed to tell Samson's friend that Samson is blood." Then Faith Ann started crying again and hung up the phone.

Curt threw his phone against the wall, shattering it into pieces. "What the fuck does that even mean," Curt screamed! He dropped to his knees. For the first time since he was a kid, not even at his daddy's funeral, Curt became to weep.

CHAPTER FOURTEEN

9th Floor, Norfolk General Hospital

Norfolk, Virginia
8 November 1968

"Hi," said Chris Mathews. "Welcome to the ninth floor." It was Chris's standard greeting to the John Does on the ward. He had known this John Doe for a while. They were smoking and checkers buddies. Sometimes they were ready to talk. Most of the time not, but Chris wasn't a Doctor, just someone who wanted to help. Chris passed a smoke out of his Marlboro soft pack. Casey took the cigarette.

"Thank you," said Casey Romain. He took the cigarette and lit it. "My name is Casey."

"Well," said Chris. "We got you down as John Doe. It says here that you won't talk to anybody. Do you have secrets?"

"I've got lots of secrets," said Casey. He took a deep inhale off his Marlboro. Then he exhaled it. Chris waited patiently for Casey while he smoked his cigarette.

When Casey had finished his smoke Chris asked, "Would you like another one?"

Casey nodded yes and Chris passed him another one. Casey did not light this one. He fidgeted around for a few moments. He would not make eye contact with Chris. Finally he put the cigarette in his pocket.

"Thank you," Casey said. "That was very good. I think I will save this for later, if you don't mind." Chris nodded that this was okay. "I was a Staff Sergeant with 5th Group Special Forces. I did two tours in Vietnam. I've been Special Forces since I was eighteen. I have seen a lot of weird shit, and I have done a lot of bad things, but bad things have happened to me too. It's kind of made me who I am." Casey pulled the cigarette out, but didn't light it. He just put it in his mouth, and continued his story.

"I met this guy on my first tour. He was a popular mercenary who fought for the South Vietnamese, but I think he would fight for whoever would have him. The rumor was that he was the eternal mercenary, a two thousand year old man who could not die. He was a Roman Legionnaire who was at the crucifixion and cursed or blessed, depending on your perception, to never die until Jesus returned for the second coming. The drawback was that he would always be drawn to conflict or warfare. It has its good points, but kind of a bummer when you stop to think about it." Casey paused and lit the cigarette. Chris passed the pack over to him. Casey nodded thanks.

"Well," Casey continued. "It was near the end of my second tour when I went on a raid with this guy again. I had been on many raids with him to include during this tour. The difference here was he caught himself a bunch of bad luck. We were going back to War Zone D. Now you got to realize that we had been to War Zone D many times before. In fact we were together for Operation Hump." Casey paused for a while, gathering himself together.

"Shit," Casey said. "It was three years ago today that we tried to take Hill 65 during Operation Hump." Casey had to stop again to collect himself. He pulled out a third cigarette and immediately lit it. "That was a real bad day," he continued. He smoked half the cigarette in silence.

"We were going back to War Zone D," Casey said while finishing his cigarette. "Just like we had many times before, but this time we were near Ben Cat. This time it should not have been like Hill 65, or anything like Operation Hump. It was basically reconnaissance. You know what I mean, like a bunch of tough boys going out camping, but we walked right into an NVA kill zone in an ambush. My old Roman friend takes about eight rounds to the head. It blew away half his fucking head! He should be dead, but he is still pumping blood. Well Casca, that's what his true warrior friends called him, had saved my life on several occasions. So I carried him out of the battle and found a place to hole up. I didn't expect him to survive, but I owed this guy big time. I was going to at least give it the old Green Beret try." Casey paused again in retrospection.

"Fuck it," Casey said, and lit a fourth cigarette. "Well, Casca's head began to grow back. I nursed him back to health. Then he began to tell me stories. It was the most wondrous time of my life." Casey relaxed, and then he began to chuckle. "He told me many stories, many, many stories, but the one I like best was about this dog. He said he cold cocked him as he was running across a field. That he initially thought of this guy as dinner, but this dog was strong. Casca actually began to like this dog. His Sergeant hated him, which caused Casa to like him even more. Then Casca releases him against his Sergeant's wish, and the dog shows up at the crucifixion of Jesus Christ. It turns out that this dog is a friend, no better, the doggie's best friend of Jesus. They die together at the cross."

"I know of this dog," said Chris. "His name is Pytre. He has just been reincarnated into human form. I was there when he was born twelve years ago. The human Pytre is completely hairless. He also has a skin disorder. He was kind of patchy, but Pytre is an amazing human being."

Casey looked at Chris and smiled. "Thanks for the smokes he said, and thanks for listening to me." Casey held out his hand and Chris shook it.

* * * * * * * *

Chris sat on the edge of his bed and chained smoked cigarettes. His grief and anguish were still very intense, but his rage had settled into a deep cold hatred. He had not even known Pytre was here at the hospital. Now his new friend Casey had murdered him. He knew he had no more aliases, but he was going to take care of business anyway. Since nobody even knew he had known Pytre, it had been easy for him to get the hospital escort duty for Casey/John Doe's transfer to the city jail. He had kept the specifics of his conversation with this John Doe a secret. No need to tip his hand.

"Well if it isn't the manager," said twelve year old Pytre. Chris leaped up knocking his ash tray and the table it was on over. You would not have been able to measure his blood pressure then because the gauge did not record that high. There before him stood Pytre, only now he had a diagonal gash across his face and a deep laceration around his neck.

"Take it easy manger," said Pytre. "It will be okay."

"Pytre," stammered Chris. "You…. You…… you're alive."

"Well," said Pytre. "Not really. Not in the mortal sense, but its all for the best."

Chris sat down hard. His head was reeling. He considered himself very open minded, but the spirit realm, kind of like death, always looked a lot different when it went from contemplating philosophical theory to staring it straight in the face.

Pytre came over and cupped Chris's face in his hands. "Don't be too hard on that Casey fellow. He was enticed into it. It was time for me to begin my teachings, and I needed to shed my mortal body. I have got to be a little quicker now. Besides, I now know what its like to be hot, or cold, or hungry, or to feel pain, or to be scared." Pytre laughed.

"Sure I never had a girl friend," continued Pytre. "But you know a lot of dogs have been spayed or neutered. I think that may be the problem with humans, they don't get themselves fixed. Then their sex drive makes them violent possessive perverts. You know that twelve years is the equivalent to eighty-four years in dog years. So now, wish me luck."

"Good luck," said Chris. He began to weep. "I love you boy."

"I love you too," said Pytre. He gave Chris a big hug. And then Pytre was gone.

CHAPTER FIFTEEN

Big Meeting Number One

Washington D.C.
20 June 2011

"You call me off the golf course to attend a meeting" said the President of the United States as he entered the Situation Room. "This had better be important." Everybody started leaping to their feet. The sound guy keyed *Hail to the Chief* on the intercom, but the damage had already been done. The President was now in even a worse mood. This meeting had started, right from the beginning, very badly.

"Mr. President," said the Secretary of Defense. "This issue is of extreme national security."

"Aren't there like a hundred thousand such matters every day," said the President, sitting down at the head of the table. The President pulled up his agenda sheet on his console. "Let's go right to the Secretary of the Navy. What is this all about?"

"Well, Mr. President," said the Secretary of the Navy. "There appears to be a potential terrorist that has been operating with total impunity in this country and world wide for over thirty years, maybe even longer. He goes by the name of Pytre Dawg. He seems to be able to elude every security system we have. We got our first clue about him in 1984, but there is a lot of evidence that he was in operation way before that. Anyway, here is a homemade security film made at an animal shelter known as the Dog Gone It." The Secretary of the Navy clicked on the video.

A grainy black and white film starts to play on the overhead and on everyone's console. There was no sound. The film showed a man kicking a dog down the aisle of an animal shelter. The aisle was lined with cages full of dogs. All the dogs appeared to be very agitated.

"This video was police evidence in Temple, Texas," said the Secretary of the Navy. "You are going to see some disturbing images. Brace yourselves."

Everyone in the room gasped. A secret service agent, who was an extreme dog lover, turned his head and let out a stifled cry of agony. It took all his effort to get himself under control. The President sat up straight in his chair.

"Now," said the Secretary of the Navy. "Enter Pytre Dawg." Everyone was mesmerized by the images. Pytre appears on camera. Pytre grabs the man's head between his two hands and snaps the man's head completely off. More gasps from the viewers. Then Pytre goes to the afflicted dog, reaches in, and holds him. The dog immediately quiets and goes to sleep. Pytre then disappears off camera. The situation room was completely silent. The dog loving secret service agent had a determined "right on" look on his face.

"Now I'm no dog lover," said the President. "But even I was disgusted by what happened to that poor dog. This happened in 1984. Granted, Rule of Law, you can't assign a death penalty for animal cruelty, but surely this is not something that needs national attention, or involvement. I mean, I'm kind of glad the guy got his just desserts. Why am I here?"

"Well Mr. President," said the Secretary. "This is one of many cases. It just the first we were able to connect to Pytre Dawg. The Owner of the shelter had set up a hidden camera that the murder victim didn't know about. He probably would not have released it except that he was briefly considered a suspect. As we started looking into this, we found many cases very similar. You probably noticed, sir that Pytre Dawg just appeared on camera, and then at the end just disappeared off camera. It is like the man can teleport. This makes him extremely dangerous. He could even appear in this room right now and kill you." Everybody looked around apprehensively.

"Okay," said the President. "Give me what else you got."

"Yes sir," said the Secretary of the Navy. He typed some commands on his console. "One thousand nine hundred and fifty six suspected cases of Pytre Dawg taking the law into his own hands since late 1968. Fifty-eight of them have been confirmed. Now he seems to be heating up. Suppose his ideology is changing and he finds fault with leaders who don't put dogs equal with man." The Secretary of the Navy looked directly at the President. "Or, suppose he is backed by a powerful terrorist organization. Let us say one that would like to take out the leader of the free world."

"Secretary of Defense," said the President. "Please give us your summation."

"Yes Mr. President," said the Secretary of Defense, standing up. "This Pytre Dawg, though benign, is a most dangerous threat. He has the power to bring you down sir. The more we learn about this guy, the more afraid we become of him. Apparently he has technology well above anything the United States has. He can appear and disappear wherever he wants. Not just on camera, but in the physical world. We can not allow that power to exist unchecked. If we can't control it, we must at least destroy it."

"Mr. President," said the Secretary of State. "We should not get involved in this. Just let the boys do their job and take care of this matter."

"Mr. President," said the Secretary of Defense. "It is a capital offense for any of us to kill a United States citizen without due process of law. We could even face the death penalty for that. Only you can issue an executive order to kill a United States citizen. We will need that in order to proceed."

"Oh just grow a pair," said the Secretary of State. "Why don't you just do your job and take care of business?"

"Madame Secretary," said the Secretary of Defense. "You have a reputation for throwing people under the bus when things go sour. I will not be tried for murder for conducting illegal operations on implied missions. You may have me killed later, but I will at least go out on my own terms."

"Whoa," said the President. "Let me think on this. You will have your orders in writing before you must act. I guarantee that. No need to rush into things on this one. It appears to me that the threat, all though real, is not immediate. Give me time. Is there anything else?" The President looked around the room. "Well, then that is all." The President rose and left the room.

* * * * * * * *

The President was preparing for bed that night. "Where is my dog," he asked?

"In the kennel sir," said the secret service agent.

"Bring him in," said the President. "I want to see him tonight." The secret service agent nodded and went to get the dog. A few minutes later there was a scurrying of feet down the hall of the White House.

"Bo," said the President. "Come here boy." Bo, the President's dog, jumped up on the bed with the President. The President cuddled him and they fell asleep together.

Several hours later, Pytre appeared at the foot of the bed. He looked down at the President of the United States cuddled up with his dog, Bo, and smiled. It was a beginning. Then Pytre was gone.

Chapter Sixteen

Dog Pound

Chicago, Illinois
2 June 1974

Fred, no middle name, no last name, had just been sworn into the Central Intelligence Agency. Fred was a nom de guerre. It was not the name he had been born with, but that was okay with Fred. He liked all that spooky stuff. He was now one of the CIA's Ghosts. He was headed off to Chicago, Illinois to investigate a young lad that could apparently walk through walls and teleport wherever he chose. Fred was excited about the assignment.

Fred put out his cigarette and cleared security at JFK. He would be landing in O'Hare in about nine hours. That gave him a little time to kill. He went into the departure bar and ordered himself a martini, shaken not stirred. Hey today, he had become James Bond. Fred took his drink and sat in a booth. He was smiling. Today was a good day.

* * * * * * * *

Tully Boswell closed up the privately owned animal shelter know simply as *Dog Pound*. The shelter's owner was a pudgy forty-five year old that had been born to wealth. The owner thought that Tully was a loser.

Tully hated his job, he hated dogs, and he really hated his boss, but he needed the money. So now he was reduced to working in a big cage full of little cages which were full of stinking animals.

"Damn it," said Tully out loud. It was that stupid mutt the pound had brought in a couple of days ago. He had escaped his cage once again. In a rage Tully took several steps and drop kicked the dog. The dog yelped as it flew through the air and hit one of the other cages. All the other dogs started barking. The dog was no stranger to pain, but the blow had stunned his back legs and now he couldn't move very fast. Tully approached the dog.

"Hey," yelled a man's voice from outside the compound. "Do not do that again." Tully looked up and saw a young man, probably a teenager standing outside the compound looking in at him. The man was hairless, hideous, and a mass of scare tissue. Tully stood up tall and glared at the man.

"This is private property," said Tully. "I suggest you leave." Tully was slightly unnerved by the guy.

"I do not want you to harm that dog again," Pytre said. He stared calmly, but intently at Tully.

Tully's rage overwhelmed him again. "Go to hell," Tully yelled. "You're pretty brave when there are steel bars and concrete separating us. These are just dumb stupid animals. I can do with them what I want. You can't boss me around. Fuck you punk!" Tully turned and raised his leg to kick the dog again.

"I would advise against that," Pytre whispered in Tully's ear. Tully spun around and shrieked. The man was inches away from him. Up close, Tully could see the massive scar that cut diagonally across his face. It also looked like someone had tried to cut his head off for there was a deep scar that circled his neck. Tully urinated himself and fell backwards on his butt. He began to whimper. Tully looked up into the man's eyes. The man's eyes were calm and kind, but there was a sense of no fooling around in them. The dogs started wagging their tails.

"Please don't kill me," whimpered Tully. He began to cry. His whole wretched life seemed to crash down and overwhelm him.

"I know," said Pytre. "Bad things have been done to you. Bad luck has befallen you. Most adults you come in contact with treat you as if you were nothing. However, when you take bad things that happen to you and pass them down to weaker or lesser beings.... well sir, you are the punk."

"Yes sir," wept Tully. "I am a punk. Please don't hurt me." Tully continued crying.

Pytre let out an exasperated sigh. He squatted in front of Tully. He waited for Tully to compose himself. Finally Tully stopped crying and looked up at the man.

"I would like to introduce you to Jack-Jack," said Pytre. "He has had a very rough life starting from when he was born in the tiny cage his mother was in." As Pytre talked Tully could see the scenes being described in vivid detail.

"He was taken from his mother before he should have been weaned," Pytre continued. Jack-Jack had come over to Pytre and snuggled up under Pytre's squatted frame. Pytre began to absentmindedly scratch Jack-Jack's belly. Jack-Jack kicked his legs in pleasure.

"He was a Christmas present to someone who tired of him within a few days," Pytre continued. "Jack-Jack was kept in a tiny cage, sometimes for days on end without food or water. He was forced to live in his own filth. He developed a phobia of cages. When he escaped, he was punished by being beaten. After a month he was abandoned by being thrown out of his owner's apartment. He tumbled down a flight of concrete stairs. He lived on the streets as best he could until the dog catcher picked him up two days ago. He does not know much kindness." Pytre looked down at Jack-Jack and rubbed him with both hands. Jack-Jack rolled on his back in delight. His hurt leg had suddenly become completely better.

"In spite of all this," Pytre said. "Jack-Jack is a kind dog. It is in his nature. Now your life and his life are entwined. What happens between you two will affect both of you"

"What?" Tully asked. "How can you make that possible?"

Pytre leaned very close to Tully's face. There was less than half an inch distance between their eye balls. "I am a dead man who walks through steel and concrete cages at the speed of light," Pytre whispered in a stern articulate voice. "Please try to stay focused here." Pytre leaned back. Tully urinated his pants a little bit more, but remained focused. Jack-Jack was wagging his tail and licking Pytre's hand.

"Picture this world," Pytre said in his soothing voice. "You and Jack-Jack are best friends." Tully once again vividly saw the images the man was describing. Pytre described a wonderful life of love. Sure there was hardship, there was also pain, but they faced it together, and with a deep love for each other. They had each others back.

"Of course," Pytre continued. "You are going to have to earn his trust now. You are the master, which is just the nature of things. That means you are going to have to do the hard work. You are going to have to make it work. Notice that I didn't say it would be nice if you did, or you ought to. What I said was you were going to have to make it work."

Pytre studied Tully intently. He sensed it would take about a week for a strong bond to be formed. He also sensed a loyal pack that would be together until death did them part. Even when Tully got married and had children, Jack-Jack would be part of the deal. Things were starting to change.

"Okay," said Pytre. "You are on your own, Jack-Jack's friend."

"My name is..," Tully said, but was interrupted by Pytre holding up his hand. Then Pytre was gone.

Tully slowly got up. He was feeling very emotional. He liked the images with the feelings they evoked, that he had seen in his head when the phantom was here telling his story. He wanted someone he could trust and love, someone that would trust him back, and maybe even love him.

"Jack-Jack," said Tully as he held out his hand. Jack-Jack bit him. Tully became mad, but quickly remembered the phantom's words, that he, Tully, would have to make it work. Tully began to laugh.

"I suppose I deserved that," said Tully. "Perhaps I can find you something a little better to eat." Tully headed off down the corridor to the lobby and offices. He went behind the counter and looked through the treats. Jack-Jack kept his distance.

"Hey Jack-Jack," said Tully. "These ones here are supposed to be nutritious and tasty. Do you like chicken?" Tully took a handful of them, put them in his smock pocket, and went back into the kennel. Jack-Jack retreated to a safe distance. Tully closed the door, sat down on the ground with his back leaning against the door. He took a chicken treat and tossed it down the aisle of the kennel to just a few feet from Jack-Jack. It took several minutes, but Jack-Jack finally came up to the treat, sniffed it, took a small bite, and then scoffed it down.

"Good boy," laughed Tully. He was having fun. He had not felt this good in a while. Tully grabbed another treat and tossed it to Jack-Jack. This time it was a just little bit closer, cutting the gap by about half. This time Jack-Jack did not wait as long to get it. Within eight treats, Jack-Jack was taking the treats out of Tully's hand. Tully was praising him and scratching on him. They played for a couple of hours, and then Jack-Jack, exhausted, feel asleep on the floor. Tully watched him contentedly, and soon feel asleep himself.

Two blocks away, on the fifth floor of the hotel, Fred put down the binoculars. "How very interesting," said Fred to his Chicago contact.

"They said you were the master of the understatement," said the Chicago contact. "We got lucky tonight. He seems to be attracted to dogs that are being mistreated by humans, but we haven't been able to trick him yet with a staged scenario."

"Fascinating," said Fred. "We did get lucky tonight. Do you think he is immortal? You know, like a ghost or something."

"Well," said the contact. "I don't know about ghosts. You agency ghosts are spooky enough for me, but according to eye witness reports, he does appear to be aging. He is aging through time in a forward linear progression, just like us regular folks, but unlike us regular folks, he appears to move really quickly and is not restrained by physical barriers. Who knows, it might be some kind of Tesla technology." The contact shrugged.

"I think I'll go talk to our witness," said Fred. "What is the background?"

"The *Dog Pound* is owned by a Mister Hiram Smith," said the contact. "Mr. Smith was born to money, lots of money, and doesn't have to work for a living. He likes dogs and so he created this no kill shelter. The witness is nineteen year old Tully Boswell. Tully was orphaned at twelve, and has had kind of a rough life. Unbeknownst to Mr. Smith, Tully has been taking his frustrations out on the dogs. Tully appears afraid of Mr. Smith, and Mr. Smith appears contemptuous of Tully. The dog is a young mutt stray picked up on the city streets two days ago. He appears to be a hard luck case also. The perfect scenario and we did not stage it. We have been keeping an eye on this place and tonight we got lucky."

"Very lucky for me," said Fred. Fred extended his hand to the contact. "I think I will take a shower, change clothes, and then pay our young Mister Tully a visit." The contact shook Fred's hand and departed the motel.

Tully awoke to the sound of someone tapping on the steel bars of the shelter. Jack-Jack was asleep in his lap. The kennel started to come alive in barking pandemonium. Tully looked over at the source of the trouble. A hardened man in a suit was standing by the bars. Tully wondered how many scary visitors you can have in one night.

"We are closed," yelled Tully at the visitor.

Fred took out his badge and held it to the bars. "Mr. Tully Boswell," said Fred. "I need a word with you please."

Tully got up and slowly approached the man at the bars. "You need a warrant to talk to me," Tully said. "Do you have a warrant?"

Fred smiled. "I'm CIA," said Fred. "Now I could come in there like your visitor did tonight, admittedly not as fast or smooth, or we can talk through the bars. The choice is yours." A touch of fear ran through Tully's body. Jack-Jack retreated to the far end of the kennel. Tully gulped, clenched himself to keep from peeing, and came up to the bars.

"Thank you Tully," said Fred. "The Agency is most interested in your visitor of last night. First, do you know his name? Anything you can tell us would be of great help."

"He didn't tell me his name," said Tully. "Not much to tell. A young man, mixed race or a skin disorder, had some scars on him, broke into here. I had to throw him out."

"I'll admit you won the pissing contest," Fred said with a huge grin. "However, I think your visitor was firmly in control of the entire encounter." Fred turned and pointed to the hotel a couple of blocks away. "I watched the whole event with binoculars from that hotel. What I would like from you is the feel of the entire visit. What was said? What appeared to happen?"

Tully was chagrinned, but decided to cooperate. He told Fred everything. Fred would occasionally interrupt to clarify a detail, but basically let Tully tell his story. It took an hour. When Tully was done, Fred extended his hand through the bars and shook Tully's hand.

"Thank you Mr. Boswell," Fred said. "Your country appreciates your service." Fred turned and left.

"Jack-Jack," said Tully. "Let's get these dogs feed. Then I got to go home and get cleaned up before my shift starts again." Tully feed all the dogs. Jack-Jack trotted along beside him. Tully finished up and looked at his watch. Three hours before he had to be back. He could make it.

Hiram Smith pulled up in his chauffeured Lincoln. He glanced through the bars at his least favorite employee. "Look at that train wreck," Mr. Smith said to his driver. "I'm going to have to fire that boy."

Tully saw Mr. Smith and groaned. Of course, after the early visitors Tully had, Mr. Smith did not seem all that menacing. Tully grabbed Jack-Jack and headed into the office as Mr. Smith was coming in.

"My God," said Mr. Smith. What are you doing here so early? Trying to milk the clock? You smell like piss. Did you just come from a party?" Hiram waited for the usual groveling and sniveling about how it wasn't his fault.

"No sir," said Tully. "I stayed here all night, but don't worry, I'm not on the clock. This little fellow is Jack-Jack. He has a wicked phobia about being locked in cages. He keeps escaping. I thought he might get hurt. So we spent the night learning how not to be afraid. We slept in the kennel, outside the cage. I think Jack-Jack might have had an accident while sleeping on my lap. Sorry sir, I'll get cleaned up and be back in time for my shift. I already fed everybody. I'd like to adopt Jack-Jack."

Mr. Smith's jaw dropped. He chocked up a little. "Of course Tully," Mr. Smith said. "You take all the time you need, and your still on the clock. The adoption will be free. I understand you don't have a lot of money." Mr. Smith reached over and scratched Jack-Jack on the head. Jack-Jack licked Mr. Smith's hand. "I remember you. You were a wild thing yesterday. Look how well behaved you are today."

Tully was leaving as the driver was coming in. "Look at that young man," said Mr. Smith to the driver. The driver nodded in agreement. Tully and Jack-Jack exited the building.

"A remarkable young man," Mr. Smith continued. "I'll think I will give him a pay raise." The driver stared at Mr. Smith in disbelief.

CHAPTER SEVENTEEN

Impromptu Meeting

Norfolk Nave Base, Virginia
23 June 2011

"Wake up sir," said Ensign Rocky Austin. He had opened the door to his guest room.

Curt rolled out of bed, he was instantly alert. "What is it?" Curt asked.

"We have been summoned to Norfolk Navel Base," said Rocky. "We are to report to the Deputy Fleet Commander, Vice Admiral Boswell."

Curt looked puzzled. "I bet it's because of that damn cell phone," said Curt. "It was government property."

"I don't think so sir," said Rocky. He looked down and did not meet Curt's eyes. "Anyway, we got to be there in two hours, which means we have got to leave here in thirty minutes. Samson is invited too. I'm going to go get ready. I'll meet you out front with the car in twenty-nine minutes. That will be zero six hundred." Rocky looked at his watch. Then Rocky went back out the guest room door leaving Curt and Samson to get ready.

At exactly 0600 hours, Curt and Samson started walking down the long sloping driveway of Rocky's house on Mayflower Avenue to the awaiting Navy sedan. Curt let Samson in the back and then jumped in the front seat.

"We have got to stop by The Hague and pick up a Commander Wayne," said Rocky. "Then off to the Navel Base. We are supposed to meet with the Vice Admiral at zero seven thirty."

Curt rode in silence, lost in his own thoughts. Rocky pulled the sedan into a circular drive way. There, in his travel dress uniform was Commander

Mike Wayne. Curt got out, held the front door open, and rendered a salute. Mike returned the salute and got in the front seat. Curt jumped in the back seat with Samson. Rocky started driving toward the base.

"I'm sorry you got pulled into this Mike," said Curt. "Seems like a lot of trouble over a secure cell phone that was destroyed, and not lost. Hell, I'll pay for the damn thing." Rocky let out a groan. Mike turned in his seat to look at Curt.

"Curt," Mike said. "What the hell are you talking about?"

"My secure cell phone," said Curt. "In a weak moment I threw it against the wall smashing it to pieces. I'm sorry, I'll pay for it." Rocky let out another moan. Mike looked from Curt to Rocky, and then back to Curt.

"According to Ensign Austin," Mike said. "He accidentally ran over your cell phone with the sedan. He pleaded guilty on the Report of Survey and is going to pay for the phone by forfeiting a whole months pay next payday."

"He's covering for me Sir," Curt said. "I'm the one that broke it. I should pay for it. Although I was not aware that he took the fall for it." Curt glared at Rocky.

"Well," said Mike. "You boys had best work that out amongst yourselves. My advice, Curt, is that you just pay Ensign Austin for the phone. When someone covers my ass, like you for instance on several occasions, I would not reward them by throwing them under the bus with possible integrity violations."

Curt reached up and put one hand on Mike's shoulder, and his other hand on Rocky's shoulder. "Thank you Rocky," Curt said. "Of course you are right Mike. I'm just not thinking clearly. This whole business has got me spooked." Mike reached up and squeezed Curt's hand.

"It's okay Curt," said Mike. "The reason we are going to go see the Deputy Fleet Commander is because Fred and the Vice Admiral apparently go way back. They want to talk to us about your friend, Pytre Dawg."

"Fred," Curt said to Mike. "I have been hoping to talk to him."

Mike chuckled. "Yeah, he said you would," Mike said.

Rocky pulled the sedan up to the front of the Fleet Headquarters building. A young sailor saluted them as they got out of the car. Rocky left it running. As they entered the building the young sailor got in the sedan and parked it in the base valet section.

They took the elevator to the fourth floor and entered the main office of the Deputy Fleet Commander. A civilian secretary was behind a desk. They could hear laughing and muffled voices behind the double closed doors of the actual Vice Admiral's office. The secretary got up and cracked the door.

"They are here sir," she said. She nodded and swung open the door. "The Admiral will see you now."

Commander Mike Wayne, followed by Lieutenant Curt Mays, followed by Ensign Rocky Austin, followed by K9 Samson, entered the Vice Admiral's office. The three human's saluted an empty desk. Samson walked over to the couch where Fred was sitting. Fred started to scratch Samson's head.

"Over here guys," said Vice Admiral Boswell. He returned there salute. The three humans joined Samson and the group at the interoffice lobby. It was made up of two couches, three stuffed chairs, and a coffee table. There were pictures of a dog all over the place. There with the Vice Admiral and Fred was Captain Dustin Martinez. They shook hands all around.

"Fred here has been filling me in on the latest developments," said Vice Admiral Boswell. "Of course, I'm getting wind of stuff from above. This has caused a rather significant stir among the big wigs, all the way up to the President of the United States. Fred, you want to bring the new arrivals up to speed?"

"Yes sir," Fred said. "Tully and I go way back, even before the Admiral here had joined the Navy. We are kind of piecing stuff together, but I guess you could say we first meet at Pytre's eighteenth birthday party." Curt was glaring at Fred and shaking his head.

The Admiral chuckled. "I guess you could say that," Tully said. "We didn't know it at the time though. What a night. Seems like another lifetime ago."

"Tell me about it," said Fred. "Anyway, that was in Chicago on 2 June 1974. That was my first official day working for the Agency, although I had worked with them for several years before that in Vietnam. The CIA had been tracking reports of a dog champion fellow, a canine crusader, whatever, who seemed to possess supernatural powers. I was lucky. My first day on the job and I get to witness, with binoculars, the encounter of our mystery man. Because of that I'm now in charge of Operation Pytre Dawg. Thanks to Curt's encounter, and the information we gained from that, we now have a name and a mortal history. We now have well over five thousand reports on Pytre sightings, not by that name of course. Probably a little fewer than two thousand are creditable, but fifty-eight are down right confirmed. Well, let's make that fifty-nine. Tully would you explain."

"Well, let's see how best to explain this," said Tully. "We are kind of a house divided on this Pytre issue. The President is on the fence on this one. He is the only one who can order the death of a United States citizen without due process of law. He is not over sensitive about killing Americans; he just isn't going to do it unless there is a good reason. Many high ranking officials think that Pytre's existence with all his abilities is all the reason needed to exterminate him. Others think that he has done nothing wrong other than take out a couple of bad guys. It is almost divided along dog lover versus non dog lover lines. The President owns a dog, Bo is his name. That gives the Pytre supporters a slight advantage. However, three nights ago, White House security cameras picked up Pytre appearing at the foot of the bed of the President while he slept. The President was with his dog. The President does not know about the Pytre visit. Another one of Fred's friends, who works in the Secret Service on the White House staff, gave Fred a heads up. He is going to try to keep a lid on this, but this stuff always leaks out. It is just the nature of things. Then we may well see an Executive Order demanding the destruction of Pytre."

"A point of order sir," said Curt. He was rubbing his temples. "Executive Order or no Executive Order, how can you kill a man who is already dead?"

"Curt," said Fred with a look of mock hurt. "You no longer subscribe to my identical twin theory?" Curt was instantly on his feet. He was shaking his finger in Fred's face.

"You don't subscribe to your fucking identical twin theory either!" Curt shouted. "You never did. When I was telling you about my encounter you acted like it was all new to you, but you knew about this guy before I was even born. Then you let me go see the manager, completely unprepared. You sir, are an asshole."

"Curt," Fred said. He had a sad smile on his face. "I owe you a lot because of Iraq. I consider you a personal friend of mine. If we were going out right now to take on a million terrorists, I'd tell you the facts straight up, but you have always had a problem with the supernatural. You have to slowly get your feet wet. I'm sorry my friend, but I had to let you do this at your own speed." Curt sat back down on the couch. Mike put his hand on Curt's shoulder.

"There are several big problems that arise if an Executive Order to terminate Pytre comes about," said Captain Martinez. He looked over at Tully.

"Go ahead Dustin," said Tully.

"Thank you sir," said Dustin. "I am a dog lover. I have eight dogs. I have never meet Pytre and did not know about him until Curt's encounter. However, I have supported K9 interactions in the military since my academy days. I think an Executive Order to destroy Pytre is bad for the following reasons. First, this will leak out and will cause havoc with our ability to track Pytre. It will become like Big Foot, or Space Aliens, with thousands of sightings a day. We will lose our focus simply because we will be overwhelmed by the numbers. Secondly, we know Pytre ages. He is not a god. There may be a way to kill him. Like I said, I never personally meet the guy, but I have grown to like him. I don't think we should kill an American citizen just because he has the potential to do harm. Thirdly, there is always going to be collateral damage. Women, children, other dogs, a lot of innocent people will die as we try to take out this one phantom. Lastly, since Pytre shows up on his own time schedule, when he wants to, and he never seems to fall for staged events, this is going to be an almost impossible mission. That means careers will be damaged and even destroyed." There were nods from all around the room.

For the next couple of hours they told Pytre stories. Fred, for the most part, dominated the conversation with his five thousand reports on the phantom dog man. Tully delighted them all with countless stories about Jack-Jack, who had lived to be eighteen. Dustin told them stories of his eight current dogs plus the twenty-seven dogs he had owned before. Even Rocky got into the act with a story about his childhood dog, a dog named Cindy, who was given to him by his father, a Navy man. Finally Vice Admiral Boswell stood up.

"Gentlemen," Tully said. He sadly looked at his watch. "This has been great, but its purpose was strictly to bring everybody up to speed. I think we all know where each other stands on this. Now if you will excuse me, I have got a luncheon with the Secretary of the Navy." They all stood. The meeting was dismissed.

CHAPTER EIGHTEEN

Dog Gone It

Temple, Texas
2 June 1984

John Casey dropped his wife off at work at the Temple Mall and then headed to his own job at the *Dog Gone It*, a privately owned animal shelter on 31st street. It was a kill shelter that held dogs for thirty days, and then in a euthanasia fashion, destroyed them. John liked his job, plus the extra income it brought in, but he hated his boss, Joey. Joey Babcock was probably sleeping with his wife. John didn't sleep with his wife, but it was a possession thing. He didn't want anyone else to have her, especially if it brought her pleasure. What John liked, was control and terror over his victims. He had done a stint in prison for forcibly sodomizing an under age young man. Now he had learned to leave no witnesses. Then he discovered that the sex act was secondary to the thrill he got from watching them suffer and die. He had become smart. He would not be caught again.

John parked in front of the *Dog Gone It*. Today was a good day; he had several dogs to put down. He was going to make this fun. He got out of the car and kicked the front door hard. The loud noise always put the dogs in a panic, and they all started barking. John Casey was ecstatic. Today was going to be great. He could feel the pain and fear in the air.

"Three of you bastards are going down," John said as he entered the shelter. He went over to the drug locker, and took out three lethal injection vials, then a fourth vial.

"Seems like one of you didn't die right away," John said. "So I had to shoot you up again. It was the humanitarian thing to do." He took the four vials put them in his pocket, and carried them out to the car. He injected all four vials into a container and put the container in a secret compartment in his car. He then took the empty vials and returned to the shelter.

"Okay," John said. "You are all dead now. My next job is to cremate your dead bodies. Who is first? John Casey walked up to a cage and read the chart, which was marked with a red tag. "Well Queen," he said, while reading the chart of the twelve year old boxer. "It is time to burn your dead body." John opened the door and dragged Queen out of her cage. He viciously started kicking Queen down the row toward the crematorium. While the dog yelped, he pushed the button that started up the fires in the furnace. Grabbing the boxer around the middle he chucked her into the lit furnace. Queen screamed as the flames caught her hair on fire and the heat burnt her paws. John was stimulated. He loved this stuff.

Pytre came up behind John Casey and put his hands on each side of John's head. With one swift movement Pytre twisted his head completely off. John Casey's body crumbled to the floor. Pytre step over him while tossing the head to one side. He walked up to the crematorium and pushed his hands through the grate. The flames licked all around his arms as he gentle touched the burning dog inside.

"You rest now Queen," Pytre said. "It is time for you to go to the next level." A blissful peace came over Queen as her spirit left her body.

The shelter was completely silent. All the dogs were staring through their cages at Pytre. Pytre turned and smiled at them, and twenty-two tails started wagging. Pytre came up to one of the cages, one of the two remaining marked with a red tag. Pytre reached in his pocket and pulled out a green tennis ball. He put it in the cage with the dog. Then Pytre was gone.

* * * * * * * * *

"So you were sleeping with the victim's wife," said Detective Lawrence. He was interviewing his only suspect down at the Temple police headquarters.

"Yes sir," said Joey Babcock. He reached in his pocket and pulled out a Beta cassette tape. "I installed a security system last Sunday on John's day off. I installed it myself. No one else knew about its existence. I had not gotten around to watching it all week. I didn't suspect anything. This is the day of the murder. It is gruesome stuff, but it shows what happened. It doesn't make any sense to me. Of course what John was doing to those dogs doesn't make any sense either. I'm glad the bastard is dead." Joey passed the cassette to Detective Lawrence.

"I'll need to see all the tapes," said Detective Lawrence. He took the tape from Joey.

"No problem sir," said Joey. "They are all very disgusting. I can bring them to you at the station or you can pick them up."

"Let's go pick them up now," said Detective Lawrence. He paused for awhile. "Ah, there is an old mutt in there that was marked to be put down today. He looks like he is mostly blue tic coon dog. He reminds me of Blue, my dog that I grew up with. We used to play fetch with this green tennis ball all the time. The dog had a tennis ball in his cage. I was wondering if ah......maybe I could take him off your hands?"

"Sure," said Joey. A really weird thought occurred to him. That was what the killer had put in the cage. Oh well, the detective will see it for himself on the film. "That would be fine sir. I will see you there."

As Joey was leaving the station he saw Sharon Casey sitting in a chair weeping. As he approached her she got up and came toward him.

"It's so horrible," she said as he put his arms around her. She collapsed against him as he held her. She was weeping uncontrollably now.

Joey continued to hold her as she cried. It was her husband who had just had his head ripped off he thought. He would have to keep her husband's deeds a secret. It was the right thing to do. Joey stood in silence holding Sharon as she wept in his arms. Finally her crying started to subside.

"It's so horrible," Sharon said. "I saw some of the tapes at the shelter. He was burning dogs alive. I'm glad he is dead. Promise me that the shelter will never kill another dog."

"I promise baby," said Joey clutching her tight. Now they were both crying.

Chapter Nineteen

Confusion and Promotion

Fort Hood, Texas
8 November 2011

"Well Curt," said Mike putting up and securing his seat tray. "If that asteroid don't wipe us all out today, then we will be back in Afghanistan by this time tomorrow."

"We can only hope," chuckled Curt. He was securing Samson into his harness. The C141 was on its final approach into Robert Gray Army Air Field. "Why are we laying over at Fort Hood? We could do an in-flight refueling. Save some time."

"We have to pick up our newest member," said Mike. "Seal Team Three is actually one member short of its assigned personnel. Besides, it will give you a chance to call Karen." Curt smiled.

The C141 touched down and taxied over to runway thirty-six. There was a bus waiting for them there. Seal Team Three debarked the plane and boarded the bus. Mike and Curt sat in the front seat. The driver went through the back gate and they were on Fort Hood.

"So Operation Pytre Dawg is on hold," said Curt. "That means we are just going to sit tight for a year until after the elections in 2012? It is going to be business as normal back in Afghanistan."

"It's a good thing Curt," said Mike. "Well it is for our side anyway. We are not going to be able to capture this guy, and have him only saving the lives of dogs of the rich and famous. No, our options are executive order to terminate Pytre, or it's on hold. I hope it stays on hold until after I retire."

"I suppose your right," said Curt. "I'm not completely politically naïve. The government cannot official sanction someone who occasionally murders United States citizens without due process of law. If the government chooses to see this thing, than they must actively choose to stop it."

The bus pulled in front of the III Corps Headquarters building. Seal Team Three exited the bus and entered the lobby of the headquarters building. An Army Captain greeted them and escorted them up the stairs to the third flour. They entered the III Corp main conference room.

Curt burst into a huge grin when he entered the conference room. There stood Karen, and she looked ravishing. He came up and gave her a big hug and a deep kiss on her lips.

"I suspect I have been picked up below the zone," Curt said. He gave Karen another kiss.

"Well sailor," said Karen. "Now that I have agreed to marry you, we can't live on the measly paycheck you've been making."

Mike came up to them and ushered them to the front of the conference room. From a side door Lieutenant, junior grade, Rocky Austin entered the conference room. In addition to his promotion, he was also wearing the Navy Seal trident.

"Attention to orders," said Rocky. He read the orders promoting Curt Mays to the rank of Lieutenant Commander. When he had finished reading the orders Mike pinned on one gold oak leaf, and then assisted Karen with pinning on the other one.

There were congratulations and hand shakes all around. Rocky was now a member of Seal Team Three and would be joining them on the flight to Afghanistan. Curt was now a Lieutenant Commander which was the authorized rank for the Deputy Commander of Seal Team Three.

"Wheels up in forty-five minutes," Mike said to the group. "Everybody needs to get back on the bus." The men started filing out of the conference room. Curt gave Karen one last kiss.

An Army Captain entered the room. "Lieutenant Commander Mays," he said.

"Right here," said Curt. The Army Captain came up to him.

"The Corp Commander would like to see you in private sir," he said. Curt looked to Mike. Mike shrugged.

"See what the three star wants," said Mike. "We will see you on the bus." Curt followed the Army Captain into a back entrance of the Corp Commander's office.

"Come in Commander Mays," said the Corp Commander. Everybody else left the room. The Corp Commander closed the door.

"My G2 just brought this to me," said the Corp Commander. "It is top secret compartmentalized. It is for your eyes only. I'm not even supposed to see it. It comes from the White House. You are to read it here and then destroy it. There is the shredder. Then you are to burn the shredded document in here." The Corp Commander handed Curt a red and white striped document. Then the Corp Commander went to the other side of his office and sat down at his desk.

Curt opened the envelope, and pulled out a one page document. The document read as follows:

Top Secret/Pytre Dog
Lieutenant Commander Curtis Mays (eyes only)
If you come into contact in any way with Pytre Dawg, you
are to bypass the chain of command and contact the White
House directly. Call the White House on a secure line. State who
you are and that this is in reference to Operation Pytre Dawg.
You will then be given further instructions.
Immediately Destroy This Document

Curt stared at the document for a few seconds more. He was confused. What did this mean? He dutifully shredded the document and the envelope that it came in. He then incinerated the shredded remains.

"Thank you sir," Curt said.

"Anytime Commander," said the Corp Commander. "Good luck in Afghanistan."

Curt hurried out the office and bounded down the stairs for the bus. As he boarded the bus he got one last glance of Karen. She was in an Army sedan, probably being escorted back to Robert Gray to catch a flight home. She blew him a kiss. He blew her one back. Next stop would be in Afghanistan.

CHAPTER TWENTY

Smithy

Leuven, Belgium
2 June 2006

Smithy jumped in his Hummer Two and sped off from the local feed store. He had over a thousand pounds of dog food in the back. It was nutritious stuff that had been approved by his veterinarian doctor. Smithy cared about his dogs. As he cleared town he rounded around a corner that bordered a castle. Smithy's family used to own that castle, but had lost it during World War Two. It now belonged to the government. Smithy began reminiscing about living there as a child. Pytre appeared in the passenger seat next to Smithy.

"God damn it Pytre," said Smithy. "Did you ever hear of knocking?" Smithy fought to control the car. One tire went off in a ditch, but he was able to drift it back on the road. He pulled the car to a stop.

"Please do not use blasphemy," said Pytre.

"I thought we were communicating," said Smithy. "You don't understand semantics."

"I don't understand semantics," said Pytre. "But, I know you were blaspheming."

"Well maybe a little bit," said Smithy. "I am sorry. You startled me. Good to see you again my friend." Smithy held out his hand and Pytre shook it.

"Ma has another pup to deliver," Pytre said. "He is twisted up in her, but with a little luck and help, he will be okay. His name will be Samson."

"Ma just had a litter three days ago," Smithy said. "She isn't doing to well. I was wondering what the problem was. What do I need to do?"

"First, pick up your comrades at the airport," Pytre said.

"They are just a couple of U.S. squids," said Smithy. "They can wait."

"No," said Pytre. "It is important that they are there. One of them bonds very strongly with the new pup, and vice versa." Smithy nodded in the affirmative. "Then, go to Ma and make sure her belly is gently rubbed and twisted. When the pup is aligned, she will go back into labor. Ma is my great-great grand daughter, back when I was a dog. That makes her litter my great-great grand kids."

Smithy laughed. "Pytre," he said. "You never could understand human mathematics."

"I understand enough," said Pytre. "There is one, then there are two, then there are three, then there are four, and then there are many. What is not to understand?"

"I stand corrected," said Smithy chuckling. "Will you accompany me to the airport?" Smithy hit the accelerator and the Hummer began to take off. He looked over at the passenger seat, and Pytre was gone. Startled he swerved the Hummer for the second time that day.

"God bless you boy," Smithy said as he got the car under control. "Blasphemy intended." He headed the Hummer toward the Charleroi Airport.

Commander Mike Wayne and Lieutenant Curt Mays were standing on the curb of the departure lane when Smithy pulled the Hummer up. They watched as the old man got out of the car.

"You're the only Yanks here," said Smithy. "You must be my charge." He gave a mock salute and opened the passenger side of the Hummer. "You will both have to get up front; the back is full of groceries for my dogs."

Mike held out his hand. "I am Commander Wayne," he said. "This is Lieutenant Mays. I understand you killed some Nazis in the war?"

"I was twelve years old," said Smithy. "I killed three Germans who were trying to hurt my mom. I also killed a French soldier and a British soldier who were trying to hurt my mom. I have never killed an American soldier, but the day is still young." Smithy looked at Mike's hand, briefly shook it, and then nodded toward the open passenger door.

"Technically," said Curt, getting in the Hummer first. "We are sailors."

"Opportunities abound," said Smithy, smiling. "I might be able to make a big dent on my bucket list. Get in boys, one of my dogs is in need of assistance."

Smithy drove the Hummer to the compound with Curt and Mike hunched up in the passenger seat. As they approached the compound, they could all see the huge entrance sign that showed nothing but a big red puppy paw.

"Hey," said Mike. "It's the University of Kentucky Wildcats. That's my Alma Mata."

"Well," said Smithy. "The Rock Hound symbol, dating back to twenty-five thousand B.C. belongs to everyone. It marks the union of man and dog. One day an asteroid will strike the moon, and the resulting crater will ensure that symbol will be seen by all mankind."

They rode in silence to the kennels. It was a large expanse covering over one hundred and forty acres. Ma's personal space was building number sixty-two. Smithy got out and entered building sixty-two. Mike and Curt scrambled out and followed him into the building. Ma was lying on her side in her special queen bed, two inches off the floor. She looked in agony. Her six pups were lying in the separated berthing room. Nurse Amy, a dog handler on loan from the U.S. Army was hand feeding them from a bottle of Ma's milk.

"She is not looking so good," said Nurse Amy. "The pups, on the other hand are doing real fine."

"Pytre said there is another pup in her," said Smithy. "We need to rub her belly and twist." Smithy went over to Ma and began to gentle rub her belly. Then he began to gently twist it. Ma moaned in pain.

Nurse Amy came over to Ma and began to gently twist her belly. "There is another pup in there," she said. "Pytre was right."

Mike and Curt, not having any idea what was going on, were still excited by the process of an underdog pup. They both came over and started stroking Ma's belly. All of a sudden, Ma groaned. She squirted a strawberry colored liquid from her vagina. Then she groaned again, shuttered, and Samson's head appeared out of the womb. Curt caught the head in his hands.

"He is a strong one," Curt said, as Samson slid into his hands, and started biting him. Mike moved over to the new pup.

"Wow," Mike said. "He is a tough one."

Ma leaned over and tried to bite the umbilical cord, but she was just too weak. She lapsed back into her prone position. Curt pulled out his pocket knife, cut the umbilical cord, and held the new pup up to Ma's mouth. Ma started licking her new son. Samson began to breath, and then wet himself. Samson then leaned over and licked Curt's hand. Curt fell in love with him.

"He is so strong," Curt said. "We should call him Samson. You know, like Samson in the bible; a strong man."

"That is his name," said Smithy. "His name is Samson."

"Yes," said Curt. "That is, if we buy him. We will name him Samson."

"No," said Smithy. "His real name is Samson."

"Yes," said Mike. "If we buy him, we will name him Samson."

"Fucking Yanks," cried Smithy. He threw his hands up in the air, turned around, and walked out of the building. He slammed the door as he left. Nurse Amy just giggled. Samson continued to lick Curt's hand. Curt scrunched Samson with his finger. Samson was only half the size of the other pups.

"I don't think he understands," said Mike. "We will name him Samson. We will buy him." Nurse Amy just giggled more. Curt wasn't paying attention. He was mesmerized with Samson.

As Samson continued to suckle on Curt's finger, Ma fell fast asleep with some much needed rest.

* * * * * * * *

They had been there a week and Curt was still mesmerized with Samson. Samson was now about three quarters the size of his siblings. He was suckling on a front teat. What amazed Curt was how smart he was to get there. At day one he would work his way into the feeding litter and bite one pup on the left leg, and the pup to his right he would bite on the right leg. Then Samson would get out of the way as the two pups would fight. Soon a litter brawl would evolve. Samson would go eat. After awhile it just became normal that the little guy would get first choice.

"Smithy," said Mike. "We will take these twenty dogs. Samson will be named Samson, and he is our number one choice. We will pick them up after your training course. Thank you." Mike extended his hand.

Commander," Smithy said, excepting the hand shake. "I will send the dogs to you after they are trained." He smiled. "I'm glad I talked you into naming him Samson." He said this sarcastically.

Mike rolled his eyes in exasperation. "Yes sir, Mister Smithy," Mike said. "It has truly been a pleasure doing business with you."

Curt came over and gave Smithy a hug. "It has been a wonderful experience," Curt said. "I envy your job."

Smithy looked at him real seriously. "You are a Navy Seal, special operations," he said. "I don't envy your job." Then he reflected on it a moment, and said, "But I do respect it. Good luck my friends. I think you and Samson will make a great team."

Mike and Curt each grabbed their bag and headed toward departures at Charleroi Airport. They were flying civilian all the way back to California.

Smithy went over to arrivals and sat down. He had a two hour wait before Nurse Amy's husband was scheduled to land. He'd be arriving in a Navy Gulf Three private courier.

CHAPTER TWENTY-ONE

Hey, Samson's Friend

KAF, Afghanistan
25 December 2011

"Merry Christmas boy," Curt said to Samson. He gave Samson a raw chicken leg and a bowl of milk. Samson dug into the treats while wagging his tail vigorously.

Samson had just finished his treats when the explosion rocked the temporary framed building they were in. Curt grabbed his sidearm. Both he and Samson exited the building and headed toward where the explosion was.

When they got there, Mike was crouched upon the south wall. Samson and Curt approached. "No bomb debris." Mike shouted. "It must be a rocket." Curt surveyed the scene. A wisp of smoke arose out of the side of the mountain as another rocket was fired at the compound.

"Yes sir," said Curt. "And they are up in the caves." Another rocket slammed into the south wall. Debris showered down on Mike, Curt, and Samson. Marines started to show up at the wall in various levels of armament. Curt fired his sidearm at the cliff, and then he handed it to Mike who was unarmed. He had a plan.

"Can you call in an air strike," shouted Mike. A third rocket hit the wall.

"Sir.... Mike," said Curt. "There is no time. Samson and I will have to take them out. I am the only one who saw where the rocket was launched. Samson has got the nose."

"He has no scent," Mike shouted. "How will he find them?"

"Samson will find them." Curt said in a calm voice. Samson looked at Curt, then at Mike, and nodded toward Mike.

"I wish he didn't fucking do that," cried Mike. Another RPG-7 Rocket hit the wall. Mike dropped to his haunches. "Okay, maybe it's a good thing. Take the armament you need Curt. Finish this. Save us. It is Christmas for Christ sake."

"You Gunny," Curt yelled. "Police me up an M203 with twelve grenades, at least four hundred rounds, and four hand grenades."

"Yes sir," said Gunny Sergeant Hawthorne. Gunny Hawthorne went to his Marines and collected the supplies. Mike and Curt went into a huddle to plan the strategy.

Gunny Hawthorne approached Curt and Mike, followed by two Marines carrying the armaments. "Here you go gentlemen," Hawthorne said. "Anything else my marines can do for you?"

"Yes Gunny," said Mike. "When Commander Mays and Samson leave out, it will be on my mark, your Marines could lay down a hell of a base of suppressive fire. Kind of gives them a chance."

"Yes sir," said Gunny Hawthorne. He turned to his men and prepared them. Another rocket slammed into the wall, which now was looking more like an ancient ruble than the most secure American compound in Afghanistan.

"On three," shouted Mike, "One, two, three, mark!"

"Reviere," whispered Curt in Samson's ear. Samson took off like a shot across the dead zone. Curt followed as fast as he could.

Under Gunny Hawthorne's control, a platoon of Marines provided a murderous covering fire on the face of the caves. No return fire or rockets came from the caves as Samson and Curt made the four hundred yard dash to the trails that led up to the caves.

Samson entered between two rocks. The trail split left and right. Samson paused at the trail fork for eight seconds, his tail up in a question mark, his head rotating 180 degrees as he sniffed the air, and his tongue licking the air as he gathered all his senses. Then his tail shot straight back and he took off to the right. Curt had caught up and sprinted after him.

Samson rounded the corner on the third tier. Seven men armed with AK-47s aimed down at him. A man on the tier below aimed his RPG-7 at Samson and fired. The men on the ledge above began firing at Samson. The rocket hit Samson on the right side of his chest, breaking two of his ribs. The rocket spun out and hit the rock face where it exploded, showering rock fragments and dust on Samson. Samson tumbled off the ledge and fell the several feet into a cavern.

Curt rounded the bend. He saw Samson get hit by the rocket and then tumble off the cliff. In a rage, Curt raised his M203 and sprayed the wall with 5.56 mm rounds. He then switched to the grenade launcher, and started pumping grenades into where the enemy was hiding. He carefully aimed each round into a cave that was facing him. When he heard a scream, Curt immediately fired a second round into the same location.

After a few minutes he heard no more screams. Curt then systematically fired a rocket grenade into each of the cubby holes, then a burst of 5.56 mm M16 rifle bullets. He waited a minute, fully exposed, and heard nothing. He then ran to the edge of the cliff where he had seen Samson disappear. He sprayed a burst of covering fire. His gun went silent. He was now completely out of ammo. It was a rookie mistake because he had gotten over emotional when he saw Samson in danger. Because he had left in a hurry, it was Christmas morning and he had not gotten the memo on the impending attack; he did not have his K-bar knife or his E-tool. He was completely weaponless except for his body.

Curt looked down over the cliff into a six foot deep ravine. It took a serpentine route to his left for about fifty feet into a rock face. No sign of Samson. To his right it took a straighter path for a couple of hundred feet into a cave opening. There was blood at the base of the cliff directly below him. That was the point he remembered seeing Samson go over the edge. Curt leaped into the ravine doing a parachute landing fall to minimize damages to his body.

"Samson," Curt called, straightening up to a crouch. He listened in silence. Not a bark or a whine could be heard. "Samson," Curt called again, this time a little louder. There was silence for about ten seconds.

"Hey! Samson's friend," said a voice from the cave. Pytre walked out of the cave and raised his hand in a wave to Curt. "Come on over here boy, Samson needs you."

Curt's heart raced. "I'm not afraid of you," Curt said in a loud and commanding voice. If there had been any mortal humans still alive on that ridge they would not have guessed that Curt was lying through his teeth. He had not been this terrified since his encounter with his dead father in Iraq, but he was here and Samson needed him. Curt remembered a wise saying his father always told him; 'You can not conquer fear. However, successful leaders, our heroes, learn to accomplish their mission while being afraid.'

Pytre looked puzzled and shrugged. "Of course not," Pytre said. "You are Samson's friend." Pytre turned and walked into the cave. His pace was quick.

"Shit," Curt said. He shoulder strapped his empty M203. He remembered another saying his daddy was always telling him; 'in for a nickel, in for a million bucks. You are either in or your not.' Curt began running toward Pytre. Pytre's form disappeared into the cave.

"Dammit," Curt muttered. He picked up the pace to a full out sprint. "I'm now trying to not be a punk ass rabbit in the eyes of a dead man who used to be a dog." As Curt's arms and legs pumped he stifled a near hysterical laugh, and thought; 'this day has probably not even started to get hard yet.'

* * * * * * * *

Mike and Gunny Hawthorne gathered up and organized the stragglers as they showed up at the wall. Mike kept glancing at his watch and looking through the binoculars. It had been ten minutes since the firing stopped, and eight minutes since the smoke cleared. All was silent on the southern front.

"Sir," said Gunny Hawthorne. "Do you want me to grab a team and go look for them? They have been gone for over twenty minutes."

"No Gunny," said Mike. "Lieutenant Commander Mays and his trusted companion do not like to be rushed. They are very thorough with their methods. Give them twenty more minutes." Mike paused and sighed. "However," he continued. "Police up a couple of corpsmen, plus a team of ten Marines, which you will lead. You, if the situation dictates will have a start time in twenty minutes. I am grabbing everybody else. We need to secure this wall now and be prepared to lay down a suppressive covering fire if needed. Give me an up when you are ready and wait for my mark. If you hear me say to the wall, that means everybody to the wall."

"Yes sir," said Gunny Hawthorne. He turned around and began barking orders at the men.

Mike mounted the wall and looked through his binoculars, scanning for any movement. He saw nothing. "Please Curt," he said. "You and Samson please be okay."

* * * * * * * *

Curt crashed through the cave entrance and stumbled, then fell down a small twenty foot decline to the back of the cave. Samson lay in a heap, blood caked on his chest, with Pytre leaning over him. Curt did a forward roll and stood up in front of them. He then dropped to a knee and leaned over Samson. Pytre was manipulating Samson's body with his hands.

"What are you doing?" Curt asked.

"His two front ribs are broken into his heart." Pytre said. "I need to move them out or they will penetrate his heart."

"What?'" Curt asked. "How can they penetrate his heart, but you have to move them, or they will penetrate his heart?"

"He is hurt bad," said Pytre. "But his first concern was for you. I had to check on you. That was his wishes. You killed all seven of them bad guys, about five times each. That is not your weakness boy. Accepting fate is. Are you okay now?"

"Yes sir," said Curt. He was ready to step through the fire. He wanted to save Samson. "What do I need to do?"

"Comfort him," said Pytre. Curt sat down and cradled Samson's head in his lap. He gently stroked Samson's head as Pytre reached into Samson's chest and healed his ribs.

Curt sat reflecting on the miracle he had just witnessed. He continued to stroke Samson's head, although Samson's health had drastically improved.

"You know," said Pytre. "Samson is my great grandson."

"You know," said Curt. "That Samson is a dog."

"I was referring to when I was a dog," sighed Pytre.

"Jesus' dog," said Curt. "Over two thousand years ago."

"Yes," said Pytre. He gave Curt a big smile and scratched Samson's side. "He is a descendent from Malika, who was a man, but also my son."

Curt rubbed his temples. Talking to Pytre was an exercise in cryptology. Then slow understanding dawned on him.

"So," Curt said. "Samson is a grandson, many times over, too many to count. He is a descendent of Malika, a favored son of yours when you were a dog. Malika was also a man who was somehow important to you, and you named this son after him."

"Yes," beamed Pytre. He gave Curt a hug. "Malika, the human, was the father of my first master, and the man who gave me to Jesus, my second master. We are communicating nicely. I will call you Warrior Curt from now on. I have only named a few other humans. Nurse Amy, Smithy, Admiral Tully, the man you call Fred whom I call by the name his mama gave him, and now you."

Curt gave Pytre a return hug. Curt, who had every medal for valor except the Medal of Honor, felt more honored than he had ever had in his life.

"Thank you," Curt said. Then his face clouded. "I'm supposed to tell the President of the United States that I have spoken to you. I think they plan to kill you."

"I'm already dead," said Pytre. "I will finish my ministries here."

"But this is the most powerful person in the world," said Curt. "He has an arsenal of nuclear weapons. He could destroy the world."

"And I would still be here along with whoever else God spared," said Pytre. "I have never met a human that had the slightest concept of what real power was. You let me worry about Bo's friend. You do what you have got to do Warrior Curt. In fact, you tell them that I will be back here, in these caves, on the fourth of July, 2014." Then Pytre was gone.

Curt got to his feet. Samson, fully recovered, heeled beside Curt with his tail wagging as Curt exited the cave. As they got to the base of the caves and entered the clearing headed back to camp they ran into a team of marines headed their way.

"Anything left sir?" Gunny Hawthorne asked.

"All dead," said Curt. "The body count is seven. Recover their bodies and search for Intel. I ran out of ammo." Curt handed his empty M203 to Gunny Hawthorne.

"Thank you sir," said Gunny Hawthorne. "You would make a good Marine sir."

Curt smiled and waved as he headed back to camp. He had to find a secure phone. He had a very important phone call to make.

CHAPTER TWENTY TWO

Ma and Company

Leuven, Belgium
2 April 2010

Colonel Amy Boswell, Army Veterinarian Doctor, Deputy Commander of the Army Veterinarian Corps, had just gotten off the phone with her husband, Vice Admiral Tully Boswell. They had been reminiscing about how they had first met in Pearl Harbor, Hawaii. She had been new to the Army then. A brand new Captain commissioned in the Veterinary Corp, because she was a Veterinary Doctor. She had gotten to skip all the food inspection jobs and go right into running a military animal clinic. Navy Lieutenant Tully Boswell, acting executive officer of the newly commissioned Ticonderoga-class cruiser USS Yorktown, had come into her clinic in a frantic manner. He was carrying his dog, Jack-Jack.

Jack-Jack, an old mutt, was very sick and feverish. Nurse Amy put him on the examination table. What she first noticed was that he had a tick firmly imbedded in his right hind leg. Removing it with tweezers she discovered it was a deer tick.

"Where has he been?" Nurse Amy asked.

"We were in Norfolk our last shore leave," said Tully. "That would have been a month ago."

"Damn," said Nurse Amy. "I think he has Lyme disease. It's very advanced." She began to draw some of Jack-Jack's blood.

"What can we do?" Tully asked. Nurse Amy was overwhelmed with this tough man's compassion for his little dog.

"The regulations say put him to sleep," said Nurse Amy. "Otherwise he will suffer."

"No," said Tully. "Life is full of suffering. We learn from it. We endure. No! We will not put him down."

"Or, we could give him a mass dose of antibodies," Nurse Amy continued. "We would have to monitor him constantly."

"Thank you," said Tully. "I will pay you for your extra services."

"Let's see how it turns out first," said Nurse Amy. She hooked up an antibiotic drip to Jack-Jack.

Around two in the morning Jack-Jack woke up and began a remarkable recovery. The blood test showed that he had indeed had Lyme disease. When Tully enquired how he could repay her, she had said that to take her out to dinner would do the trick.

The next night at dinner, Tully had absentmindedly mentioned Pytre. Nurse Amy was instantly in his face.

"Describe Pytre," said Nurse Amy. Tully realized by her wild eyes that he was going to get kissed or murdered in the next few minutes. Truth was always the best policy. He gulped, and then took a deep breath.

"Multi-ethnic fellow, pretty scared up, loves dogs," Tully timidly said. "Oh, and he is a ghost." He won the kiss instead of being murdered. She told him how she had met Pytre. They ended up making love that night, and were married a month later.

Colonel Boswell's memories were interrupted by a loud explosion. She jumped up from her chair and ran to the door of her apartment. Scanning the compound, she saw a large column of smoke and flames coming from where building sixty-two was.

"Shit, that's Ma's run," said Nurse Amy. She grabbed the keys to her hummer and drove over to that area. As she approached the now destroyed and burning building, she saw Smithy's Hummer out front. It was parked, but still running. She leaped out of her vehicle and headed toward the building. A second explosion rocked what was left of the building. Smithy staggered out the front door. His left arm was missing at the shoulder. Blood spurted from the wound. He fell into her arms.

"There are still some to save," Smithy gasped, and then died. Nurse Amy tightly clutched him for a few seconds. Then gently lowered him down, and ran into the building.

Pandemonium abounded as Nurse Amy entered the building. Dead mangled dogs and dog body parts were strewn all over the burning building. In the back of the building, just before the door to the run, lay the birthing room. Ma's still, lifeless body lay on the floor. Two of the pups were still alive and clinging to their dead mother.

Nurse Amy grabbed the chain link door to the birthing room and immediately yanked her hand back. The cage door was red hot. Taking off her blouse, she wrapped her hands and grabbed the door again. It would not budge. Pulling with all her strength, she slowly dragged the door open. The pain was intense as the door burnt her hands through the material. The room was getting very smoky. She was choking on the fumes. Entering the room, she cradled up the two puppies in her badly burnt hands and exited back the way she came. The smoke was so bad now that she had to get down on the floor and crawl.

Nurse Amy did the Army low crawl with the two puppies cradled in the crux of her forearms. The smoke was starting to settle to the floor now. She did it one movement at a time, fighting to remain conscious. Elbow forward, then knee forward, then elbow forward, then the other knee forward, and then repeat the whole process. The entrance door, with its fresh air and safety was still about twenty feet away. Summoning all her strength, she moved forward, one movement at a time. The smoke was strangling her. At five feet from the door, her reserve exhausted, she lost consciousness.

Nurse Amy's mind drifted back to the time she had first met Pytre. She had been a little girl of six then. Her parents had been killed in an automobile accident two months earlier. She was living with her Aunt and Uncle, who had Cindy, a black Labrador. Cindy had just given birth to eight cute little puppies two days before. This morning, Cindy had been hit by a car and killed. Just like Amy's parents had been killed, by a car. Amy was devastated and focused all her attentions on taking care of the pups. She had fashioned baby bottles from her doll set and hand fed all the pups. On the fourth day, one of the pups died. Amy's Aunt and Uncle decided that it would be better to put the pups down. They talked to Amy about doing the right thing. They told Amy that the pups were suffering and would not survive without their mom. Amy cried herself to sleep with the seven remaining pups clutched to her body. She awoke with a very odd looking young man, one who looked like he may have been in a car accident himself. He was sitting in a chair beside her bed, and was working on her baby bottles. He told Amy that his name was Pytre, and gave her detailed instructions on how to save the remaining seven pups. Amy followed the instructions, and Pytre visited her every night for two weeks. On his last visit, Pytre told her that he had decided to call her Nurse Amy because of the excellent way she had nursed the puppies back from the brink.

Colonel Boswell awoke on the ground outside of her vehicle. The two puppies she had saved were cuddled in her arms, just like that night so many years ago when she had first met Pytre. Coughing, she cradled the puppies closer. Pytre crouched down beside her.

"Hello Nurse Amy," Pytre said. He gave her a very warm smile. "Good to see you again. Still saving the little ones I see. Great! I appreciate that. Your hair was on fire when I dragged you out." Pytre patted the side of her head. "I put it out, but you might want to go to a, ahhhh, what did Madame Mystic call it, ohhhh, a hair dresser. I've never been to one so I can't really relate. I also appreciate the fact that, once again, when you were in trouble, you tried to handle it. You did not try to summon me like some kind of demon. You are my friend Nurse Amy." Pytre stood up. "Also, even though the wires were cut, I set off the fire alarms. Help will be arriving soon. The firemen seem like good people. They are Spot's friends. I trust Spot and so should you. They will be here shortly. Another thing, there is no one left alive in there, don't let more people get killed trying to find more bodies until the fire ends, and the third bomb goes off."

Nurse Amy looked up and gave a weak smile to Pytre. "Thank you," she gasped. Pytre bent and kissed her head. Then he was gone.

Spot lead the four firemen from the Leuven Fire Brigade Engine truck, up the slight embankment to the burning building on the rise. He circled around the hummer and led them straight to Nurse Amy and the two pups. Spot gave one loud bark. The first responders were there in seconds.

"Got one over here, and with two puppies," said the fireman, and also a paramedic, Sven Hall. His team joined up with them and they performed life saving operations on both Colonel Boswell and the puppies. "She is coming around."

Nurse Amy awoke again to Spot licking her face. "You must be Spot," she said. The four first responders gathered around her. "There are no more survivors in there, and another bomb may be going off in a few minutes. Please don't go in there. And take care off these puppies." Sven slapped an oxygen mask on Nurse Amy.

"Don't send anybody in there," said Sven. He put the loops of the mask over Nurse Amy's head. Nurse Amy again lost conciseness.

* * * * * * * *

"Attention on deck," said the senior Nurse at the United States section of the ERMC hospital in Belgium.

"Carry on," said Vice Admiral Tully Boswell. He was carrying a bouquet of flowers he had bought at the gift shop down stairs.

"Follow me sir," said the senior Nurse. "Your wife is in a private room in the corner. Well, not really private. She shares the room with two other patients. Their names are Sammy and Chewy."

Tully smiled. He followed the nurse into a room where his wife was sitting up on the bed playing with the two puppies she had saved from Ma's run.

"Hello beautiful," said Tully. He sat the flowers on the table next to her. Amy looked up and beamed.

"My hair is a mess," Nurse Amy said. She put the puppies down in a box beside her bed.

"You don't have any hair," said Tully. "But you are still, as always, beautiful. The doctors said your hair would grow back, and you would have full use of your hands again. My wife, the hero, dodges another bullet. I love you Nurse Amy."

"I love you too Admiral Tully," said Amy. "It was Pytre that saved me."

"I figured as much," said Tully. "However you are still being put in for the Army Soldier's Medal by the Secretary of the Army, based on the strong recommendations of the Leuven Fire Brigade. It seems a third explosion took out the rest of the building. It would have killed all of the firefighters if you had not intervened. Plus everybody is mightily impressed with your abilities as you saved the puppies and got out of the building. I am also mightily impressed, and once again, I owe Pytre."

"Pytre put the fire out on my head," said Amy. "And Smithy is dead." Amy began to weep. Tully sat on the bed next to her, and cradled her in his arms. He let her cry herself out. As he looked down at his wife's bandaged head and hands, Tully realized what a lucky man he was to have her.

A commotion broke out on the floor under their feet. The two puppies were scrapping. "What have we here?" Tully asked. He scooped up the two dogs from their box. One started biting on his hand. He handed the other one to Amy, who was smiling again.

"This must be Chewy," said Tully scratching the head of the puppy that was still gnawing on his hand.

"Yes he is," giggled Amy. "He is very appropriately named. This one here is Sammy. He is extremely bright. I named in honor of his much older brother. A dog named Samson that I got to help deliver about four years ago. Samson was another extremely bright dog. Samson is in the Navy now."

"Wow," said Tully. "I thought you said he was smart." Amy punched Tully in his arm with the back of her bandaged hand.

"Tully," Amy said. She hesitated a moment. "I'd like to keep these two. Not as service dogs, but as family. We have not had a dog since Jack-Jack passed."

"Than it shall be done Nurse Amy," said Tully. He bent and kissed her on her bandaged forehead. "Besides, it will be good for the kids. Sara was too young to remember Jack-Jack. It is time."

"I love you Admiral Tully," said Amy. She kissed him on the lips. Their kiss lingered for several moments.

"So where is this Samson stationed?" Tully asked.

"One of the Seal Teams," said Amy. She looked up in Tully's eyes.

"When you say he is a smart dog," Tully chuckled. "I believe you are remarking on his ability to grasp situations rapidly in a dangerous situation, and not any reference to common sense in a survival sort of way." Nurse Amy giggled, and kissed Tully again on the lips.

The senior Nurse was walking by and stuck her head in the door. "I'll just close this door to give you all some privacy," she said, and then winked as she closed the door.

CHAPTER TWENTY THREE

Executive Order 622014

Air Force One, 35,000 feet over Kansas
2 June 2014

"Mr. President," said the Congresswoman from California. "He is a threat to National Security. He must be destroyed!" She slammed her hand down on the desk top. It came down a little harder than she intended because Air Force One made a slight dip in altitude at that exact same time. The President jumped but then regained his composure. They were in his Executive Office, the top deck of Air Force One. There were only five people in the room, and the office was in secure mode. They could not be monitored.

"As far as we know he has only killed one person," said the President. He was using his soothing voice. "And that was a man who used to burn dogs alive. It was also thirty years ago. So he loves dogs. We tolerate a lot more radical groups than that."

"But he comes and goes whenever he likes," said the Congresswoman. "Even in very secure areas like the White House, and the Capital. Anyone of us could be murdered in our sleep. Hell, he has shown up next to your bed on three occasions. That is three occasions that we know of because we caught them on film. The Secret Service was totally oblivious until after the fact. In the one murder that we know of, he ripped a man's head off with his bear hands. He is a threat to National Security, and to all of us. Now, thanks to that Seal Team guy, we now have a chance to stop him for good."

The President sighed and put his head in his hands. "I don't know," he muttered.

"Mr. President," said the Vice President of the United States, getting up from a chair in the back of the President's office. "This isn't just about you, although you are a primary concern with this man, but all of us are at risk. Dogs are just animals. If one of us were to support a bill that put humans over dogs, well that could trigger this guy. If we could catch him we would. However, we don't know how he gets around like he does. We must take this one shot, and terminate this guy. It may very well be our only shot."

The Secretary of State was looking very agitated. Finally she stood up. "I am not a dog person," she said. "Yes, I've owned dogs, but people are what matter to me. I find dog lovers to be as backward in their thinking as religious people. That makes them very dangerous. As you know, I plan to be the next President of the United States. I would hate to think that my views on dogs cost me my life, and this country the life of its President. This guy, Pytre Dawg, is only one man; because of his abilities he is very dangerous. He must be destroyed." She remained standing, glaring down at the President. There was only one more person in the Executive Office of Air Force One. The President swiveled his chair around.

"Fred," said the President. "I would like to hear your thoughts on this matter."

Fred collected his thoughts, and then stood up. "As you know, Mr. President, I have been the case officer on Pytre Dawg since the beginning. I know I have been protective of him in the past, but I have had a change of heart. His abilities to appear and disappear are great. We don't know how he does it or how to stop him. We have information, thanks to Lieutenant Commander Curt Mays, Deputy Commander of Seal Team Three, which will give us a chance to stop this potential threat. It may be our only chance to do so. I think it is a matter of National Security that you sign the Executive Order. I mean, better safe than sorry. It is only the life of one man. Weigh in the balance that if we don't, we could lose the life of a great leader, or leaders."

"Okay," said the President. "Let me see the order." The Vice President went to his open brief case and extracted a large folder. He pulled out a smaller Red and White striped folder from the larger folder, and retrieved a single sheet of paper. He turned it around and placed it on the desk in front of the President. The President read in silence:

Executive Order 622014.

It is ordered that the person know as Pytre Dawg, born on 2 June 1956, in Norfolk, Virginia, be terminated with extreme prejudice. He is a threat to the National Security of this country. Intelligence places him at or near the caves surrounding the Kandahar Air Field in Afghanistan on 4 July 2014. Navy Seal Team Three will coordinate this termination. It is a need to know mission only. If unsuccessful, these orders will no longer be in effect.

The President nodded. "So," he said. "If it gets screwed up, and you don't kill Pytre Dawg, then the orders are off until you get my permission again. I like that. How do we spin this to the public?"

There were several gasps in the room. "This can not leak," said the Congresswomen from California. "Not before or after."

"This should be on the down low," said the Vice President. "You are having a dog loving, American citizen executed because he is better than our Secret Service at getting around in secure places. How do you think your distracters would spin that?"

The President glanced over at Fred. Fred nodded. "Better play this one very close to the vest, Mr. President," Fred said.

The President glanced around the room staring each person in the eye. Then he pulled out a pen from his jacket pocket, and signed the order.

"It is approved," said the President. He handed the signed order back to the Vice President who put it back in the folder and returned it to his briefcase. The Vice President then nodded to Fred.

Fred got up and walked to the office door. He went to flip the switch to unsecure.

"Fred," said the President. "I want to be kept in the loop."

"Yes sir," said Fred. "We will put you on a secure video feed like we did with the Osama bin Laden raid. You will be able to watch it in real time." The President nodded.

Fred turned and switched the lever to the unsecured position. He then exited the Executive Office and headed to the communications room. He had a lot of coordinating to do.

CHAPTER TWENTY FOUR

The Hit

KAF, Afghanistan
4 July 2014

Curt raised his hand. He was standing against the back wall of the Hot Ops briefing room at KAF. Commander Mike Wayne stopped his briefing. He looked concerned.

"Yes Curt," said Mike. While he waited for Curt to respond he nodded to the Master Chief to start passing out the CEOIs which contained all their codes, call signs, and radio frequencies.

"I don't think Samson should go on this mission," said Curt. Curt fidgeted and looked down.

"Agreed," said Mike. "I was going to let you make that call. That means you must be the one to positively identify Pytre Dawg."

Curt nodded in the affirmative and looked up at Mike meeting his gaze directly. "It is best this way sir," said Curt. Curt looked down at Samson who looked back up at him quizzically. Samson was wearing his new collar that Karen had given him with the Silver Star he had received just a month earlier freshly embroidered on it, along with his other awards, and the Trident K9 Warrior emblem. Curt reached down and scratched his head.

Mike continued with his briefing, giving assignments to the Marine Rife Platoon, The TOW Rocket squad, and the Four Deuce (4.2) Mortar Squad. He also gave coordinating instructions to the Air Force Liaison for the A-10 strikes. When he was done, he turned to the Presidential Liaison.

"Ready when ever you are sir," said Mike. The Presidential Liaison turned to his console, said some things into his headset, and clicked on the feed.

The President of the United States appeared on the big screen. "Men and Women of our Armed Services," said the President. "You are embarking on a great mission to keep free and secure this grateful nation. I personally appreciate your dedication and sacrifice. I will be watching you on a live feed. Your country depends on you. I wish you God speed and good luck." The screen went blank.

The men started to file out to their positions in the field. The start of operation would be in two hours. That gave them some prep time, but they had to be in position by start of operations. This was being monitored by the Commander in Chief. This had to go right. There could not be another Operation Eagle Claw. That had cost a President his job, and a political party twelve years of power. This would never make the papers, but it would still cost careers. Everybody was tense.

"Curt," yelled Mike. He walked up to his deputy commander. "I need you on station in one hour. I agree with your decision about Samson. You know what you've got to do. Take the time now to spend with Samson before you put him in a time out status. Rocky will take over your chores until then, but in one hour, be on station and in charge.

"Yes sir," said Curt. He saluted Mike, and walked to his quarters. Samson fell into stride beside him. They entered Curt and Samson's temporary efficiency quarters. Curt opened his refrigerator and grabbed a raw chicken leg and an opened quart of milk container. He gave the leg to Samson, and poured the milk in Samson's bowl.

Samson took the chicken leg, and waited for Curt's permission. "Well of course," said Curt. "After all, according to the U.S. Navy, it is your official birthday. Enjoy yourself my friend." Samson ate the chicken leg savoring every bite, then went over to the bowl of milk and lapped it all up. He then crawled up on the couch next to Curt, and laid his head on Curt's lap. Curt scratched his head for twenty minutes. Then Curt stood up and walked to the door. Samson got up and followed him.

When he got to the door, Curt turned to Samson. "Daek," said Curt. Samson stopped, backed up, and sat down. He looked at Curt in total bewilderment. "Not this time boy. Daek." Curt did not have to repeat the word to stay for Samson, but he did it for himself. Samson obeyed his orders while Curt closed and locked the door. He debated over locking it, but then considered that the lock was for humans, not dogs. Curt headed to his position on the caves, and awaited the mission.

Curt passed Mike heading out of the compound gate.

"You okay?" asked Mike. He was looking at Curt with real concern. Curt was looking detached. Mike grabbed Curt by the arm. "We need you on this one. It has got to succeed," said Mike. "The dog days are gone."

Curt looked at the feed and said, "I agree, we must do this. National Security depends on it." Mike nodded in the affirmative. They both headed out of the gate. In the background you could hear Samson howl.

Curt walked into the mouth of the caves. "I am here," Curt said. He held up his hands in mock surrender. Then Curt stayed perfectly still, and waited. Ten minutes went by. Finally, at twelve minutes past Curt's arrival, Pytre appeared at the mouth of a cave just above where Curt was standing.

"Warrior Curt," said Pytre. "Wait right there. I'll come down to you." Pytre started to scale down the side of the cliff. When he was half way down the cliff, Curt removed his hat. This was the signal that he had made a positive identification, and the team was to engage the target.

A single shot caught Pytre in the back, followed half a second later by dozens of other shots, all of them finding their target. Curt turned and took off at a run. He had sixty seconds before the missiles and mortar rounds came.

As Curt sprinted to safety he thought to himself that it was very fitting that Pytre was shot in the back. Curt was starting to feel a little disillusioned about the way his country sometimes did things. Curt rounded the corner to safety.

Pytre tumbled into the cavern. A TOW missile hit his body and exploded. Seconds later, three four deuce high explosive mortar rounds landed on Pytre's mangled and destroyed body. From his perch atop the command vehicle, Mike ordered a cease fire over the radio. Curt headed back to the kill zone with a small body bag to pick up what was left of Pytre. A DNA analysis would be done, and compared to the one on record from the restaurant.

Half a world away, in the situation room of the White House, a cheer went up from a small group of witnesses. The threat had been eliminated. Fred stood up.

"Once the DNA results confirm the identity," said Fred. "I will destroy all records referring to Pytre Dawg. This never happened. Pytre Dawg never happened."

The President nodded. "Thank you Fred," he said.

CHAPTER TWENTY FIVE

Down the Rabbit Hole

Damascus, Syria
2 June 2014

Curt ran after Samson, who was running after the Syrian rebel that had been taking pot shots at the village children from his sniper perch. That was until Samson had sniffed him out. The sniper had managed to kill three young children that day before Samson could get to him. Samson had so surprised the man that he had left his rifle, and took off running.

Within twenty seconds, Samson had closed the distance and administered the bite to the rebel's left leg. The man let out a scream as he went down. Samson held firm with the bite until Curt arrived, huffing, several seconds later.

"Braafy Samson," said Curt. "The intelligence people want one alive." Samson released the man from the bite and moved back out of Curt's way. Samson sat, but remained vigilant. The man reached under his tunic and pulled out a revolver.

"Don't my friend," said Curt in a soothing voice. "You don't have to go there."

The man cocked the hammer and put tension on the trigger. Curt shot him in the head with his M16.

"Damn," said Curt. "Taking one of these guys alive is the hardest assignment I've had in my whole Navy career." Curt rapidly searched the body, then threw the man over his shoulder, and headed back to the sniper perch. Samson fell into step beside Curt.

When they got to the perch, Curt laid the body down, and started searching the area. Samson barked. There was a loud click. Samson hit Curt hard with a full run lunge that toppled Curt to the prone position. Samson lay on top of Curt. The explosion from the IED sent shrapnel flying just inches over their prone bodies. They lay that way for several seconds. Curt reached up with his left hand and gentle scrunched Samson's ears and the back of his neck.

"Braffy Samson," Curt said in a slightly shaken voice. "You are truly the best dog in the Universe." Curt slowly disentangled himself, and got up. Samson shook his fur out, and sat looking up at Curt.

Curt surveyed the area. The blast had opened a hole in the foliage growing over the rock face to the east of the sniper perch. Curt pushed against it and it yielded. Curt lost his balance, and tumbled through and into the hidden entrance to the cave. He continued to tumble down a long corridor and into a small room at the back of the cave. The IED blast had weakened the cave entrance's structure. Curt's tumble was the final straw, and the cave entrance collapsed putting Curt in total darkness except for a small rock hole window, about one foot square, at the back of the cave. Curt looked through the window, and had a beautiful view of the city of Damascus.

Curt could hear Samson barking like crazy outside the sealed off cave. Then he heard a muffled male voice, and Samson went quiet.

"Warrior Curt," said Pytre striking a match, and lighting a candle in the corner of the room. The dim light revealed a primitive room with bed roll and some meager provisions.

"Ahhh! Pytre," said a very startled Curt. "Damn it man. You are the reason I am going to have heart trouble in later life."

Pytre smiled. "Good to see you my friend," Pytre said. He held open his arms. Curt embraced him.

"It is good to see you too," said Curt patting Pytre's back. "Is Samson okay?"

"You are trapped in this cave," said Pytre. "I have sent Samson to go get help from your friends. It will be awhile. I thought we could use this time to talk about the future."

"Sure," said Curt. "I told the President of the United States about our meeting on Christmas a couple years back. You suggested I do that. I hope that doesn't back fire on you."

Pytre smiled at Curt. "Bo's friend has just signed a parchment ordering that I be killed at our next scheduled meeting," said Pytre. "He has directed that your pack, your warrior team, be the ones to kill me."

"We won't do it," said Curt. "I'll resign my commission first, or you could just not show up that day in Afghanistan."

"I prefer we stick to original plan," said Pytre looking Curt directly in the eyes. "Kings and Queens have always been under the illusion of power. It's what makes them tick. As long as they think I am alive, they will remain scared. They will interfere with my ministries. They will cause grief to those I minister to. If they think I am dead, and that it would be bad for their image if people were to find out that they killed me, then they will not interfere with me. They will officially do all in their power to prove I don't exist. The bad guys in the know will lie and cover up. The good guys in the know will be thought of as kooks. It will be similar to Bigfoot and UFO scenarios."

Curt's jaw dropped. "So," Curt said, and then paused for a second. "You are saying that Bigfoot and UFOs are real?"

Pytre sighed and rubbed his forehead. "Please try to stay focused," Pytre said. "I am not saying that Bigfoot and UFOs are real. I wouldn't know the answer to that. That is not my mission. I was just giving examples of how the system works. Focus Warrior Curt." Pytre poked Curt in the chest with his finger.

"Yes sir," said Curt. "Sorry."

"When I was attached to a mortal body I was killed," Pytre continued. "I can not be killed again because I am not attached to a mortal body. I create this body when I appear, out of the surrounding elements. When I disappear, the body goes back to the elements, unless I choose to leave parts of it behind, but my spirit does not remain in those physical parts." Understanding dawned on Curt.

"We could kill your physical body," said Curt. "Your spirit would leave, and could reappear in another physical body, but we would still have the first one to check DNA and even do an autopsy."

"Yes," said Pytre. He was smiling again. "Then the Kings and Queens would leave me alone. In fact they will go out of their way to insist that I never existed in the first place. The believers will be left alone and thought of as kooks. I will be able to finish my ministries."

"It is a genius plan," said Curt. "I am in, and will do my part. Thank you for saving Samson. He has saved my life on numerous occasions. If you don't mind me asking, what is your mission?" Pytre got a studious look on his face.

"I am to foster good will between man and dog," said Pytre. "A great cataclysmic event divides the people of Earth. It will leave a mark visible to all of mankind. It will be a reminder that man and dog can work together for the common good. The symbol is called the Rock Hound. It is the impression a puppy's paw print would make on the ground. It is an ancient pre-historic symbol used by early man to identify dog friendly people. They used to etch it into the rock at the entrance to their caves. It was recognized by both man and dog. The Rock Hound will one day be visible from Earth on the surface of the moon. It will be a reminder of the covenant."

"Wow," said Curt. "Will I live to see this?"

"I do not know," said Pytre. "My ministries will end before the event, but I do not know the time of the event, just that it will be."

Pytre was gone. Curt could hear Samson barking outside.

"Samson," Curt yelled. "Braafy!"

"Commander Mays," someone shouted. "Are you in there?"

"Yes, This is Commander Mays. I am in here and I'm okay."

"Stand back from the entrance sir," the voice shouted. A platoon of Marines started removing debris from the entrance. Within half an hour they had freed Curt.

"Hell of a dog, sir," said one of the Marines to the freshly rescued Curt.

"Yes he is," said Curt. "He is the best dog in the world." Curt was loving and scratching all over Samson.

When they got back to the base camp, Curt went directly to his Team Leader, Commander Mike Wayne's quarters.

"Mike," said Curt. "We have got some serious talking to do." Nine hours later, when the sun was starting to come up, they were still in serious conversation.

CHAPTER TWENTY SIX

Christmas Party

Ranchita, California
25 December 2014

Curt opened the gate to his favorite outdoor café, a still very dog friendly place called *Rock Hounds*. Samson trotted through the gate, sat down, and obediently waited for his master to enter. Curt walked in and shut the gate.

"Déjà vu," said Curt. "This is where my life completely changed three and a half years ago." Curt waved to everybody. "Merry Christmas!"

"Karen," shouted Nurse Amy. "Your husband is here." Karen came out caring a huge plate of ribs.

"There are my two favorite men," Karen said, a big smile broke out on her face. She sat the ribs down on the table, and gave Curt a big hug and kiss. Then she bent down and scratched Samson's head.

"Go play," said Curt. Samson took off for where Sammy and Chewy were tugging against each other on a chew toy. Curt gave Karen another hug and kiss, and then walked over to his old boss.

"Captain Mike Wayne," said Curt. "The new Chief of Staff for Vice Admiral Tully Boswell." The two men shook hands.

"Warrior Curt," said Mike. "I tried to get you frocked so you could take command of Seal Team Three, but some things not even a three star admiral can do. Even though you have been acting commander for two months, you do not have enough time in grade. I'm afraid you will have to break in another boss."

"Well I hope I do as well as I did with you," said Curt. "It has been a real pleasure Mike." Admiral Boswell walked up to the group.

"Merry Christmas Warrior Curt," said Tully.

"Back at you Admiral Tully," said Curt. Sam the owner of the establishment gave a wave to Curt from across the room. He was setting up pitchers of beer and bowls of milk on the counter. He also set up a pitcher of milk.

Mike was starring straight at him when Pytre materialized right in front of him.

"Ahhh," said Mike. He spilt his Solo Cup full of beer. "I believed my friends when they told me, and I saw the videos with my own eyes, but I was not prepared for that."

There were shouts of 'Pytre,' and 'Merry Christmas' from around the room. All the dogs had stopped playing, and gathered around where Pytre stood.

"Merry Christmas everybody," said Pytre. He raised both hands in the air, and gave his iconic charming smile. "Happy Birthday to Jesus." There were cheers all around.

Curt grabbed two plates of ribs and followed Karen to a table. She was carrying a bowl of milk and a pitcher of milk. Curt gave a low whistle, and Samson trotted over to him. Curt put the bowl of milk on the floor, and handed Samson a rib. Samson dug in. Karen returned with a pitcher of beer and three glass mugs.

"Glass mugs," said Karen. "Only the best for us." Pytre approached the table carrying a plate of ribs.

"Hello my friends," said Pytre. "Do you mind if I join this table so I can spend Christmas dinner with my great-grandson?"

"Not at all Pytre," said Curt standing up. "I think Karen was expecting you." Karen poured a mug of milk, and handed it to Pytre after he had sat down.

"Thank you," said Pytre. "And Congratulations Karen and Warrior Curt, you both are going to make great parents."

Karen's eyes got real wide. "I haven't told him yet. I don't even know myself. My doctor's appointment isn't until after the holidays."

"So," said Curt. "You know if my wife is pregnant, even before the doctor does, but you don't know if Bigfoot is real?' Pytre was chuckling.

"What is your obsession with Bigfoot?" Pytre asked. "You should be happy with the news I just gave you."

"I'm just saying," said Curt. "Now that I'm a certified kook, who commits high treason against the very country he has sworn his life to protect, I think I have a right to know. You know what they say, in for a nickel, in for a million bucks. I believe all this stuff now. Why won't you tell me?"

"What has Bigfoot have to do with anything?" Karen asked.

"Your husband and I were having a very important conversation in Syria a while back," said Pytre. "We were talking about important world changing events. I accidentally led him off task with a casual remark about Bigfoot. Bigfoot is like a giant squirrel to him. If there is a Bigfoot in the area he can not stay focused on the task at hand. Remember that Karen when it is time to deliver that baby. Make sure there are no Bigfoots in the area or you will lose the support of your husband."

"You son of a bitch," said Curt. "It is a reasonable request." Pytre was roaring with laughter now.

Ting-ting-ting went Sam, the owner, by tapping a butter knife on his glass. "May I have your attention please," Sam said. "It is a family tradition in my pack to sing Christmas carols at Christmas dinner. I would like to ask our guest of honor if he has a preference."

"I love singing Christmas carols," said Pytre standing up. "I used to do that as a child with Madame Mystic. Oh, I know. My favorite Christmas carol is *Old Dog Trey*."

Curt was laughing now. He leaned over the table, and whispered to Karen, "I am so off the deep end."

"Isn't it a great place to be," Karen whispered back.

As Pytre started, the whole group joined in on the Stephen Foster song. Even the dogs were howling. Everybody was having a really good time. Even Fred was laughing.

CHAPTER TWENTY SEVEN

Fred

Langford, BC, Canada
27 December 2014

Fred reviewed the security tapes from the Christmas party of two days ago. They would be quite valuable to many higher ups in the system. He had been ordered by the President of the United States to forward any information he came across that involved Pytre Dawg. Fred chuckled as the group started singing *Old Dog Trey*, the dogs howling along. Fred took the tape out when it had finished playing and put it into his shredder. He then took the shredded pieces and burnt them in his office incendiary. He was tired of doing the work for kings and queens. He was doing this for himself and his friends. Who knows, maybe it would get him right with the lord.

"Thank you Casca," said Pytre. He put his hand on Fred's shoulder. Fred did not flinch. His heart rate did not even increase. Fred reached up with his hand and placed it on top of Pytre's hand, and gave it a squeeze.

"My pleasure old friend," said Fred. "We didn't start off on the best of terms, back when you were a dog, but over the centuries, I have grown rather fond of you."

"You are Pytre's friend," said Pytre. "I am Jesus' friend. I think your time here is coming close to an end. You will be able to move to the next level soon."

Pytre was gone. A single tear fell from Fred's eye, a tear that had been over two thousand years in the making. Casca finally felt good about himself.

THE PROFESSOR SERIES

THE PROFESSOR

The Anti-Semitic and The Jew

Thirteen year old Brandon Hale stood outside the window, in the cold Rochester air. He looked in at the old Jew bitch. The cold only added to his rage, and it was damn cold. Even for upper New York.

It was eight o'clock on Halloween night, and the temperature had already dropped well below freezing. The old biddy didn't even have trick or treat stuff up, as if she were too good to participate in the sacred tradition of giving kids candy. Well then, no treat, then a trick, and he had a great trick for her.

Brandon was certain she was the one that had squealed on him. Someone had squealed on him, and it sure wasn't Tom, his best friend. Besides, those Jews were always squealing on regular folks. She was supposedly a Holocaust victim. Tom's cool older brother, Jim, had told Brandon that there was no Holocaust. It was just a cheap Jew conspiracy to gain sympathy, and to make money. Those Jews love their money more than they do us regular folks. Well tonight, old Finkelstein, that is old Frankenstein as the cool kids called her, would pay. As soon as she went up to bed, he would smash out all her windows. Brandon smiled, for the first time that night, as he thought of all that cold air, plowing in through the broken windows of her old, run down, little townhouse.

Brandon reached into his paper route bag, and pulled out one of the biscuit sized rocks. Anytime now, he thought. Inside, just like clockwork, Anna Finkelstein glanced at the clock, put down her knitting, and headed upstairs. When Brandon heard the upstairs bedroom door close, he waited ten minutes, and then heaved the rock through the downstairs window.

121

The glass shattered. There was some more sound of breaking glass as the rock continued on its path, and knocked over a table lamp. Grinning madly, Brandon reached for another rock, and then, everything went silent. The falling glass stayed suspended in mid-air. It was like the whole world froze in place. A cat walking down the alley stood stock still, paw raised to make the next step. A startled pigeon was suspended in mid flap, hovering, but perfectly still. Brandon whirled, as he heard a voice behind him.

"Hello, my name is Professor Emit N. Relevart," said a bearded gray haired old man in a rumpled tweed suit. "You must be Master Brandon Hale."

Brandon, in a panic, let out a shriek, turned, and sprinted into a trash can. The pain was the worst he had every felt.

"I'm here to educate you," said Professor Relevart, helping Brandon up. "My lesson was to be on history, and learning how to get along in society, but for your safety, we will take a sidebar into physics."

Brandon, dazed, was rubbing the sore spots all over the left side of his body. He no longer held thoughts of escape, but resigned himself to a meek acceptance of whatever fate this strange, powerful man held for him.

"When living in a four dimensional universe," continued the Professor. "It is imperative, that when you are suspended in time, you do not run into stationary objects. It will hurt like the dickens."

Brandon nodded, and started to cry. He couldn't stop the tears. He felt like he was six again, the last time his mom had hugged him.

"You're a good kid, deep down," said the Professor. "You just need to be educated so that you can make the right decisions in life. It is not that you will make all good ones, nobody does. I'm just trying to keep you from making really bad ones. Since nobody else has taught you, I will. You have won a scholarship, seeing as how you come from a poor family."

"We're not poor!' Shouted Brandon. "My dad is the plant foreman. He makes six figures a year."

"I meant poor spiritually, little Brandon," said the Professor, tousling Brandon's hair. "When was the last time you did, or even witnessed a good deed? When was the last time you went to church? God has an equal opportunity program. Because you live in a deprived, spiritually speaking, family, you will receive this education free of charge. Are you ready to learn?"

Brandon nodded meekly. The Professor put his arm around the boy, bowed his head, and muttered a prayer. Brandon blacked out.

* *

Anna Finkelstein closed her bedroom door and sat in her favorite rocking chair, thinking about Mauthausen. She had been very reflective today and wasn't sure why. It probably was seeing that boy in the supermarket today. He was the spitting image of Brandon, but Brandon was most probably dead. Even, if by some miracle he had survived Mauthausen, he would be in his seventies now. The resemblance was uncanny.

Anna shook her head, trying to clear the memories. She hated thinking about the past. The past held only pain. She had been happy enough in early 1938. As an eighteen year old newlywed, she had been a proud member of her community, living in the same apartment complex as her parents, grandparents, brother, his wife, Uncle Jon, and her baby brother. She was a Hungarian Jew, but in early 1938, that didn't hold any special connotations. Less than one year later her whole world had collapsed. She and her whole family were uprooted and moved to the Theresiensfadt Ghetto. By the time she was herded off to Auschwitz, in the winter of 1942, she had witnessed the murder of her entire family. Her husband had been the last to go, and he had died of starvation. He had sacrificed most of the food he received to keep her and her baby brother alive. Starvation is a horrible and slow death to witness, and then, as if by mockery, they had grabbed up her baby brother one day, and just shot him.

Anna wept into her hands, shaking her head back and forth, and rocking rapid little half rocks. For months she had kept the past at bay. Numbness was much preferred to the pain, but that boy today, he looked so much like the boy from Mauthausen. She remembered she had been an animal when they railed her out of Auschwitz, numb, soulless, and scared. Most of that time period was a blur, thank God, but she remembered thinking on that cattle car ride that it can't get any worse. That was before Mauthausen, and Mauthausen was definitely worse.

They say the good thing about the medical experiments, and tortures at Mauthausen, was that it kept you out of that damn quarry. On little to no rations, inmates were required to dig stone out of the ground with rudimentary tools, and carry them up to the top of the quarry. This was done twenty hours a day. For fun, the guards would force inmates to line up at the top of the quarry and leap to their deaths. This rock-faced cliff was known as *Parachutists Wall*. Anna had been there a couple of weeks when she decided that a leap from the wall would be her only salvation. She had been struggling up the side of the quarry with a boulder. She sat it down, and started walking up toward *Parachutists Wall*. If the guards saw her, they would either force her to jump, or shoot her. If they did not see her in time, she would jump on her own accord. Either way, the madness would stop soon. A peace, one she had not felt in years, fell over her body as she approached the top.

Then Brandon had appeared. He was so petrified, but there was also that spark of life in him, that had been driven out of most inmates long ago. Brandon was still human, still clinging to life. Anna grabbed him, turned around, and headed down to the bottom. They had not been seen.

She remembered that Brandon could not speak a word of anything but English. They had spent six months together in that hell known as Mauthausen. He had been terrified the whole time, and had clung to her. She on the other hand had gathered strength from helping him. Once again, she had allowed herself to care about someone. Then the day before they were liberated, Brandon had just disappeared. He had disappeared as fast, and mysteriously, as he had appeared. Anna vowed never to care about anyone again, and for fifty-five years she had kept that promise.

A loud crash, followed by the sound of shattering glass, woke Anna from her reverie. Putting on her shawl, she rushed downstairs. At her age this took a couple of minutes.

"My Lord," she muttered as she noticed the rock amongst the carnage of her living room. She heard a sound outside. It sounded like a young boy crying. Anna went out to her porch.

"I'm sorry. I'm so very sorry," wailed Brandon. He was on his knees and doubled over in grief.

"Did you do that?" Anna asked. The boy just kept repeating how sorry he was. Anna stared hard at him. It was the boy from the supermarket. It was her Brandon look alike. He was obviously in great duress. Maybe it was her thoughts of this evening, or maybe she was just a crazy old lady. Anyway, against her better judgment, but in complete agreement with her heart, she opened up her arms. Brandon ran to her, and fell sobbing into her arms.

* *

Brandon was running when he left school and headed for Aunt Anna's house. He was going to play a trick on her. He grabbed her trashcan and headed around to the side of the house. Putting the trashcan up in its slot, Brandon did his best to put on his most solemn face. Looking down he headed back to the front porch.

He glanced up to see Aunt Anna looking quizzically at him. He couldn't help it, and broke into a big grin, then losing the battle completely, started laughing.

"Honor roll?" Asked Aunt Anna, as she looked at the teenage boy rolling on the ground laughing.

"Straight A's," gasped Brandon between laughs. He couldn't help it. He was always so happy around her. He had also been very emotional, but in a good way, since his lesson with the professor.

"Well get up boy," said Aunt Anna. "You knew you couldn't fool me. I've already baked an apple pie to celebrate." Anna turned to go inside, and then said over her shoulder, "Did you tell your folks yet?"

"No Aunt Anna. Not yet, but I will. I get along good with them now, thanks to you." Brandon followed her into the kitchen. "Aunt Anna?"

Anna turned and looked at him. "Yes Brandon."

"I love you," Brandon said, and gave her a big hug.

"I love you too," said Anna, a little misty eyed. She had re-realized the joys of caring for someone.

* *

In a dimension humans are not familiar with, Professor Emit N. Relevart, took out his little black grade book, and opened it to the page which contained the names Anna Finkelstein, and Brandon Hale. By each name he marked an A. He then turned the page, looked at the information it contained, smiled, and closed the book. His next assignment was in San Francisco, in the year 1972.

THE PROFESSOR TWO

Sergeant Jimbo and the Band of Love Children

Sergeant James Malone buckled his seatbelt as the Flying Tiger Jet Airplane started its final approach into San Francisco. He was returning from his tour with the Eleventh Armored Cavalry Regiment, in Vietnam. At nineteen, he had been scared to death when he received his orders sending him to Vietnam. Now, a few days passed his twenty-first birthday, there was a sense of accomplishment, coupled with a blissful calm. It wasn't that he had survived combat. That was more luck than anything else. It was more the fact that he had overcome his fears, and helped a lot of people. Not only Americans. His hand absently rubbed the Silver Star Medal on his chest. He had saved Americans also, to include his Commanding Officer in a fire fight outside of Bien Hoa. That had won him the Silver Star. There was also that crazy band of hippies. Sergeant Malone smiled. They had no business being in Vietnam. But, the medal didn't mean much to him. What made him content was his help to the Vietnamese people, specifically the Hamlet Trung Hung.

"Seat backs up," the pilot commanded over the intercom. "We are two minutes out, on final. Welcome home soldiers."

A cheer went up among the passengers. Sergeant Malone pulled his seat into the upright position. The intercom crackled for a second or two, as if keyed up, but no one was talking.

"I'm proud of you guys," continued the pilot. There was another pause. When he came back on he seemed choked up. "I'm afraid you won't receive a very warm welcome in San Francisco, but I want you to know that I respect, and appreciate all that you have done. God bless you."

Sergeant Malone smiled as he contemplated the stunned silence. It seamed strange, and also very ironic, for they had not received a warm welcome in Vietnam either. His thoughts drifted back to the Hamlet Trung Hung.

His troop had saved the Hamlet from certain destruction when they had counterattacked an ARVN raid. He had saved even more lives when he insisted that wounded Vietnamese civilians be medically evacuated, and treated. One of these was Vu Cat's mother. That was how he met Vu Cat, the eight year old boy, who had coined his nickname, Sergeant Jimbo. That was eight months ago, and now, just about everybody who knew him called him Sergeant Jimbo.

"Sergeant Jimbo," said Lieutenant Beckerman, tapping him on his arm. "Let's go. You are the last one on the plane. We don't want to keep those lovely American women waiting."

"Yes sir," replied Sergeant Malone as he grabbed his kit bag, and headed down the aisle in front of the waiting Lieutenant. He was in no hurry. There was nobody waiting for him here. He had a mother that lived in Peachtree City, Georgia. He would see her tomorrow. She was planning to meet his plane when he landed at Fort Benning. There was also his high school buddies, but he had changed so much since the last time he had seen them. Being with them would be awkward, to say the least. No, he was not in any hurry.

"Good luck with the rest of your life, Sergeant Jimbo," said Lieutenant Beckerman, extending his hand.

"Thank you, sir," said Sergeant Malone, shaking the Lieutenant's hand. Good luck to you too, sir." Beckerman wasn't a bad sort, as far as officers went.

"Got to go," Lieutenant Beckerman said. "Wife is waiting for me." He turned, and ran down the gangway.

* * *

"Where's Shank?" asked Sexy Susie. She was tired of having to mother hen these guys.

"Toking up with Peace and Tommy," said Vicky in a hurt voice. "I was coming to get you to see if you wanted to join us."

Sexy let out a sigh of exasperation, and fought to maintain control. Vicky was always on the verge of tears lately, she was probably pregnant again.

"Look," said Sexy in her most soothing voice. "The fascist pig, world dominating, oppressors are landing another plane of baby killers over at the airfield in Oakland. We have to get ready for the rally. Can you take me to them?"

Vicky nodded. She was sniffling now. Sexy gave her a hug. Why can't they stay more focused? Vicky, at twenty-two, was almost two years older than her, but Sexy was the undisputed leader of the group. It seems like now all they wanted to do was get high, and Shank, the one who had recruited her, was the worst of them all now. Well, it was time to do her duties as mother hen.

"The Band of Love Children will stop oppression," chanted Sexy squeezing Vicky's hand.

"And make the world free for love," chanted Vicky. She was laughing now. That girl's mood could change more times in a minute, than she changed boyfriends in a week.

She found Shank, Peace, and Tommy stoned out of their gourds back at the pad. None of the protest signs had been made.

"Sexy Susie," said Shank as she entered their one room pad that slept all five of them. At five foot, two, and one hundred twenty pounds, she considered herself fat, not sexy. It must be that she had down to her ass, long blonde hair, and big tits that made her sexy. That appeared to be what the guys cared most about. They sure didn't care about her keen intellect, motherly nature, and concern for world politics. Hell, they hadn't even done one letter on the protest signs.

"The signs aren't done," she said.

"Relax, Sexy," said Shank. "The world will be here tomorrow for us to save. Have a hit."

"No it won't," she snapped. "You let the ink dry on this brush." She was close to tears now, and getting mad. They didn't understand how important this was.

"Don't be uptight," cooed Shank. "Take a hit. I think you really need it."

Sexy took a small hit, and the group seemed to relax. It did make her feel a little less uptight. All was not lost. She could still make crude letters with the dried up brush. She painted all five signs herself.

* * *

With eight hours before his next flight, Sergeant Malone decided to take a look around in the San Francisco Bay area. Before joining the Army, he had never been out of Georgia. After Vietnam, he couldn't see enough places. He thrived off visiting different cultures. His theory was that all people had some good in them, no matter how different they may appear on the outside. He had never been to San Francisco, and the opportunity may not every present itself again.

Sergeant Malone checked his kit bag into a locker, and exited the base into the warm muggy streets. He took a deep breath, and drank in the aroma. The place was teaming with activity. His smile broadened. He loved life, and it was moments like this that heightened his since of appreciation. Look at all those people, all those different types of people, living together in peace.

He noticed a group of about five protesting hippies, carrying signs, and chanting. He gave a quick double take. They looked like the group he had saved in Vietnam. Then he chastised himself. They all look the same to me. He hated that term. It didn't mater if you where referring to the brothers, the Asians, or a group of freedom loving hippies, the term was still hateful. He felt ashamed, but still, they looked so familiar. Sergeant Malone decided he had to get a closer look.

"The Band of Love Children will stop oppression," chanted the young lady with long blonde hair. She did look like Susan, and her voice was similar. Only this girl's voice was harsher, and more forceful.

"And free the world for love," replied the other four in the group.

Sergeant Malone approached staring quizzically, his smile frozen on his face. The leader of the group spun around, and glared at him. The sign she was carrying had the words Baby Killer crudely painted in bold black letters. Her face was contorted in rage.

"Baby killer!" she screamed at him. She then bent down, and picked up a paper cup. With one deft motion, she threw its contents, hitting him squarely on the medals on his chest. It splashed up into his face, and he was bombarded with a strong urine smell.

"Get the baby killers out of Vietnam," she spoke directly at him. Her voice was choked with hatred, and rage. She lifted her sign up over her head.

"Get the baby killers out of Vietnam," she said again, and proceeded to bring the sign down on top of his head. The others were chanting behind her.

Sergeant Malone lost it. He had not cried his whole time in Vietnam, but all this hatred and rage on such a peaceful street overwhelmed him. A whole years worth of grief came bubbling out, and he began to sob. They were deep soul wrenching sobs that he couldn't control. He couldn't even make an effort to ward of the blow.

The blow never came. After a moment he looked up. She was frozen in front of him. Her face was a mask of rage, but unmoving. Disbelievingly he looked around. Everybody was frozen still. Make that everything, for the cars, buses, trucks, birds, cats, and even a windswept newspaper were frozen stock still. Nothing was moving. Had he lost his mind?

Movement caught his eye, and he turned to see a bearded gray haired old man in a crumpled tweed suit approaching him. He was carrying a towel, and a steaming mug.

"Sergeant Jimbo," the Professor said. Their was deep affection in his voice. He handed Malone the towel. "Clean yourself off."

Sergeant Malone took the towel, and started to dry his face. Everywhere the towel touched instantly became clean. It even got rid of his five o'clock shadow, and polished his medals.

"For you," said the man. He handed him the mug, and took back the towel. "French vanilla coffee, with one cream. I believe that is your favorite. Just the way your mom makes it."

"How did you know that?" asked Malone.

The man broke into a hearty laugh. "I love you mortals," he said. He gave Malone a hug. "I just froze time, and handed you a magic towel, but your concern is how I knew what your favorite coffee was."

Malone started to laugh too, although his was border line hysteria.

"My name is Professor Emit N. Relevart. I work for God. It's kind of an angel thing. I help people that are on that point of singularity where their lives can go in one of several directions."

"And my life is at that," Malone paused for a moment. "Point of singularity?"

"No, no, my boy," said the Professor. "I just wanted to say hi, and cheer you up a bit. My business is with your friends, well specifically Susan. You'll do fine in life. Sure, you will make mistakes, and there will definitely be those hard times, but you'll handle things okay, albeit imperfectly."

"What do I do?" asked Sergeant Malone. He was calming down now.

"Just have a seat over there, and relax." The Professor hesitated a moment. "I appreciated what you did in Vietnam. You helped a lot of people. Not all soldiers are like you." He gave a smile. "When you finish your coffee, the world will go back to normal. Movement will return. I'm afraid I'll have to take my mug back, it will disappear on you."

Malone nodded.

"Goodbye, Sergeant Jimbo," said the Professor extending his hand. "I hope you will maintain your positive outlook on life."

He then disappeared. Sergeant Malone looked around for a brief moment, and then headed to the bench the Professor had indicated. Sitting down he began to drink his coffee. It was as good as mom's.

* * *

Sexy Susie had just thrown a cup of piss on the baby killer. He had the nerve to smile at her while wearing a uniform full of stripes and medals. It was the last straw on a stress filled day, and it put her into a rage. How dare he approach her like that, as if they where friends. He probably wanted to rape her. She was going to bean him in the head with her sign. She lifted it up to hit him. She could hear the others chanting behind her. They were in the spirit of it now.

"Get the baby killers out of Vietnam," she said, as she brought the sign down on top of his head.

He was gone. He just disappeared. The world was spinning. Now they were in the woods somewhere. Some type of jungle. Maybe she shouldn't have taken that hit of Shank's pipe after all. No telling what was in it.

"What the hell?" She heard Shank's voice behind her.

Vicky began to cry. "Where are we?"

Peace and Tommy walked in front of her, their eyes wide.

"Far out," said Peace. She squeezed Tommy's hand. They walked off down the trail in front of her.

"This is a good trip," said Tommy. He and Peace intently watched a monkey skitter across some upper branches.

Sexy managed to round them all up about the time a small oriental boy came running down the trail. He stopped when he saw them, and shouted something in a foreign language. It sounded like, "Have a coke with Robert E. Lee." That didn't make any sense. What had Shank given them.

The small boy was talking again. "Americans?"

Sexy nodded. Oh, God, she thought, get me out of this trip. Sexy always hated being stoned. This had come on so suddenly. One moment she was okay, bashing in the head of some baby killer, and the next she was in a jungle talking to a small oriental boy.

"You come, bad guys on the way," the boy was saying. He was tugging at her arm now. "Quickly, Charlie almost here."

She was dizzy, but slowly starting to understand. They were in Vietnam. Someway, somehow, they had been transported to Vietnam. Maybe God was giving them a chance to bring peace to this war torn country.

"Its okay," she said to the boy, then turning to the group. "Come on Band of Love Children, we have a mission from God."

They starred at her as if she were insane.

"Lady, you got to go now," the boy said, and started running down the trail.

"The Band of Love Children will stop oppression," she said, and held her fist up in the air. The group did not respond. They still looked at her as if she were crazy. "Follow me. We will free the world for love." She took off after the boy. The group followed. You could hear mortar rounds landing, coming from the other direction.

As she caught up with the boy she yelled. "Stop. We can bring peace to this region. No need to run or fight."

"Lady, you crazy," was his response.

The others had caught up, stopped, and gathered around her. They were looking at her quizzically. She felt the exhilarating zeal of her mission, a mission from God. She would save the world.

"Today Vietnam, tomorrow the world," she said, and raised both arms in the air. A man wearing black pajamas appeared at the far end of the trail. She looked down the trail at him. "Don't worry my friend, we are all on the same side here. We will help you. Together, we can stop oppression."

He raised up his rifle, and shot her. It hurt real bad.

* * *

Sergeant Malone slowly drank his coffee. He starred intently at the blonde haired girl, frozen in time, her sign suspended in an ark to crash down on his head. It sure looked like Susan, but that would be insane. Of course, it was no crazier than anything else that had happened today, or this whole year for that matter. His mind drifted back to Vietnam.

Vu Cat had come running up to his track. "Sergeant Jimbo! Sergeant Jimbo!" Behind him came a group of….. hippies. They were carrying a wounded girl who had been shot in the chest. Her white cotton dress was soaked in blood. "She shot!"

Sergeant Malone, track commander, and senior medic was instantly out of the track. "Set her here." They laid her next to the vehicle, and backed off. That was good. At least they wouldn't get in the way. He quickly checked her vitals. Stable, although her pulse was rapid. Her collar bone was shattered. The bullet had hit her in the upper right part of her chest. It had not only shattered her collar bone, but took off part of her shoulder. She was moaning something.

"I was trying to bring peace," she moaned. "Why did he shoot me?"

"There are no politics on the front lines," he said without thinking.

She looked up at him, and starred for awhile. Finally she smiled. "It's you."

"Yep, it's me. What is your name?" He was rapidly applying first aid to her. Not really listening to her.

"Sex..," she gasped, then looked him in the eyes for a while.

He felt it hard to concentrate while she was starring at him. She had very beautiful eyes.

"Susan," she said.

"Well, Susan, it will be okay. You will live, although you will have a pretty nasty scar. What are you doing here?

"Trying to save the world," she gasped. "Kind of silly, aint it?" She gazed at him with those deep blue eyes.

"Not really," he said. "That's the same reason I'm here." They starred into each others eyes. There was a spark of understanding that passed between them.

Sergeant Malone turned to Vu Cat, and in Vietnamese said, "Ask Lieutenant Beckerman to call a dust off." Vu Cat took off toward the Hamlet Trung Hung. Malone then turned his attention to Susan, and began to comfort her.

Three hour later, Warrant Officer Steve Earl landed his Huey helicopter on LZ Bravo. Malone was waiting for him with Susan. The others had mysteriously disappeared.

"Sergeant Jimbo," the pilot Steve Earl said. "What you got for me?"

"She's been shot in the chest, sir," said Malone. "An American."

"Civilian?" Earl asked.

"Yes sir," said Malone.

"You got orders?" Earl asked, smiling.

"No sir," said Malone, looking at he ground.

"Wow," said Earl. "Didn't see that one coming. Load her up. Besides, this betters my odds." He gave Malone a wink.

Malone quickly loaded Susan into the helicopter. After she was secured he asked. "What odds are those sir?"

"Well," said Earl in his Texas drawl. "Half the Regiment says that Charlie will kill me before you get me court martialed. Being the intelligent man that I am, I figure, that if I'm dead, I can't collect on the bet. So I'm betting heavily on the court martial." Warrant Officer Earl pulled pitch, and the chopper rose up in the air. He gave Sergeant Jimbo a wink.

Malone looked up at the chopper, smiled, and rendered a salute. He winked back, and mouthed the words, thank you.

* * *

Sexy Susie, or Susan, as her parents called her, passed out as the chopper lifted off. She awoke in a cloud filled world. An old gray haired bearded man in a crumpled tweed jacket was sitting next to her.

"Hello Susan," he said. "My name is Professor Emit N. Relevart. Would you like me to stop the pain?"

Susan nodded. She felt calm, and at peace.

The Professor leaned over, and touched her wound. It immediately stopped hurting. "I'm sorry you had to go through this, but I think it will be a benefit in the long run. I work for God, it's an angel type thing. Your friends, the Band of Love Children, have already been returned. Would you like me to take the scars away?"

Susan thought of the battle worn, and scarred face of Sergeant Jimbo, the man who had saved her. "No, it will help me remember."

The Professor looked at her and smiled. "I had a feeling you would say that." When he removed his hand, her wound had healed by six months. It was still a nasty red scar.

"Thank you," she said, clutching his hand.

"The privilege is mine, Madame Senator," he said. "I must now return you."

"I understand," said Susan. As she faded into unconsciousness she mouthed the words, thanks. In the next moment she was smashing her protest sign into the empty pavement where Sergeant Jimbo had been standing.

* * *

Sergeant Malone had finished his cup of coffee, and true to the prediction, the cup had disappeared. He looked over in the direction of the girl in time to see her smash the sign into the pavement. Her face had changed now. She was more peaceful looking. As she came up from the blow she looked around, panic stricken. She was crying like he had been. She saw him, and broke into a smile.

He made contact with those beautiful blue eyes, and had to smile back. It was Susan. What a day this had been.

"Sergeant Jimbo!" Susan screamed as she came running toward him. She caught him in a giant bear hug, and planted a giant kiss on his lips. "How can I every repay you?"

"Well," said Malone, a little off guard. "I've got six more hours here. Can you give me a tour of San Francisco?"

Taking his hand in hers she gave it a squeeze, and said, "I think I can do that soldier boy." As they walked off down the street, the Band of Love Children gave out a loud cheer.

* * *

Professor Emit N. Relevart took out his little black book, and turned to the page with her name on it. By her name he marked an A plus. In parenthesis, next to it, he wrote, year 2008, Susan Malone elected to U. S. Senate. He closed the book, and put it in his pocket. He had one more stop to do today, and that was in Killeen, Texas, in the year 1984.

THE PROFESSOR THREE

Smoking and the Single Mom

Beth expertly wheeled through traffic using her left hand as she lit her cigarette with her right. She had three minutes to pick Karen up from school, and two hours before time to start her second job. She had done this drill every school day this year, and had become quite expert at it.

"You're so good," she said aloud as she pulled into the school lot just as the bell rang. She lit another cigarette, and let out a plume of blue gray smoke, relaxing for the first time since six o'clock this morning.

"Hi Mom," said Karen. Beth waited patiently for the ritual to unfold. Karen opened the back door of the car, put her back pack in the seat, then locked and closed the back door, and opened the front passenger door and got in. She did not say a word until her seat belt was properly fastened, and tightened, intently concentrating on every action.

"Good girl," said Beth. "How was school today?"

Karen looked up, and smiled. "Fine Mom," she said. "We learned that President Regan was also a movie star when he was younger. Our teacher, Ms. Anderson laughed, and said he was still playing a movie role. We also learned to play *Three Blind Mice*, on the potato flute." Then her face became studious as she observed her Mom take another drag off her cigarette. "We learned in Health class today that smoking is bad for you. It is unhealthy. If we know someone who smokes we should urge them to quite. Smoking can make them sick, and they could even die from it."

Beth exhaled another plume of smoke while giving an exasperated sigh. "Sweetheart," Beth said as she batted some smoke with her hand. "That doesn't apply to single moms who have to work two jobs to make ends meet.

If Mommy doesn't smoke, Mommy goes crazy. And if Mommy goes crazy, she takes a lot of people with her. Understand?"

Karen nodded. She had a quizzical expression on her face. She didn't really understand, but she knew better than to argue with that statement. "Yes Mom."

"I'm taking you to Nanny's today," Beth said as she exhaled smoke, consciously aiming for the open window. "I'll pick you up after I get off work."

Beth finished her cigarette and fought the urge to light up another cigarette. It was only five minutes to Nanny's house. She could wait to light up until after Karen was gone. She pulled up behind a pickup truck at a red light.

Beth looked out her window at an Army soldier, pushing a baby stroller, his wife clinging to his arm, as they walked down the sidewalk. They were laughing and talking. It made Beth a little envious. She had often wished she had a family. A mother and father, a husband, the normal things everybody else seemed to have. She let her gaze drift behind them.

Suddenly she jerked her attention back to the soldier family. They had frozen in mid stride. Beth wheeled around wildly, everything was motionless. Karen sat starring ahead, not moving, Karen was not even breathing. Beth took her foot off the brake, and hit the accelerator, at the same time trying to turn the wheel hard to the left. Nothing moved. The brake remained motionless in the depressed position.

"Hi Bethy," said a familiar voice.

Beth turned and looked into the face of her mother. "Mom," she sobbed. Her eyes filled with tears as she thought back to the last time she had seen her mom alive. Beth was only sixteen when her mother had finally succumbed to lung cancer. It had been a horrible year, for everybody. Beth had been filled with such rage and confusion. She had dropped out of school, and run away from home. A year later she found herself smoking three packs a day, and pregnant with Karen. She never regretted Karen, but life had not been easy for her after that.

"There is someone I want you to meet," said her mom. Her eyes were also full of tears. There was a bearded, gray haired man in a crumbled tweed suit standing next to her. "This is Professor Emit N. Relevart," she said gesturing toward the strange man. "He works for God; it is kind of like an angel thing."

"Please to meet you Beth," said the Professor, extending his hand.

Beth shakily took it. "What have you done to Karen?"

The Professor smiled. "Well, technically nothing," he said. "She and the rest of the world are going through life, business as normal. You on the other hand, have been taken out of the time space continuum. That means that the world appears to be frozen, or completely still … from your perspective. Let's take a walk, relatively speaking."

Beth found herself floating upward, next to the Professor, and her mom.

"I'm sorry sweetheart," said Beth's mom, as they floated into a cloud. "I wish I could have been a better role model."

"Mom," Beth said. She was starting to cry again. "You gave me love, and I loved you."

"Sometimes that's not enough." Beth's mom moved next to her, and they gave each other a hug. They were now completely engulfed in the clouds, but they could still see each other.

"We all have a high respect for the love in this family," said the Professor. He had moved in next to the hugging couple, and they were now standing upright within the clouds. "That is why you are given this opportunity to break this vicious cycle."

Beth's mom gave a knowing look. Beth stared at him uncomprehending.

"I am going to show you three scenes," said the Professor, touching Beth's arm. "Three events, one of which is in the past, and can't be changed, but two are in the future. They will happen if the current course goes unaltered. However, with your effort, they might have a better outcome."

The Professor gave her a compassionate look, and squeezed her arm. "It will be a hard lesson, but one that if learned, will be well worth it. Are you willing to do this?"

"It is very, very important," said Beth's mom. She was crying again.

"I'm scared," said Beth. She was nodding her head in the affirmative.

The Professor gave her a smile, "A common state of being for mothers." He waved his hand, and Beth was sixteen again. She was at the hospital, visiting her mom. It was her first visit.

"Hand me my cigarettes, girl," her mom was saying. She was struggling to get out of the hospital bed. "Walk with me outside."

"Mom," whimpered Beth. "Don't you think you shouldn't smoke? I mean with your illness, and all."

"The doctors aren't really sure what causes this," Mom said, putting the cigarette in her mouth as she walked down the hall toward the atrium. "Besides, if Mommy doesn't smoke, Mommy goes crazy. And if Mommy goes crazy, she takes a lot of people with her. Understand?"

Beth didn't really understand. Why did her mom have to be sick and away from home in the hospital? Why had her dad left? Why was life so hard?

Beth watched as if she were watching a movie in fast forward mode. Except she was aware and remembered ever sensation, every nuance, as it occurred. As the year and her mother's illness grew, so did her confused anger. She became mad at the world, and herself.

"I'm sorry you had to go through that," said the Professor. They were back in the clouds. Beth and her mom were both weeping.

"I'm so sorry too," said her mother. She was tightly clutching Beth.

"I needed the pain to be fresh," said the Professor. He looked like he was also hurting. "Most people have a tendency to rationalize. This makes that harder to do that. Are you ready to continue the lesson?"

Beth looked into her mothers tear streaked eyes. Her mother nodded at her.

"Don't make the same mistake I did," her mother cried.

Beth gave her a hug, and whispered, "I love you." She then turned to the Professor and nodded her agreement.

"This is the way things are scheduled to be on the current unchanged course," said the Professor. He gave Beth a smile. "Maybe these lessons will give you the strength to change things." He gently touched Beth's arm.

Beth was at a funeral, her funeral. It was not well attended, as expected. She had not been big on, or had time for friends, but she instantly recognized one person in attendance. The crying teenage girl had to be Karen. She looked so young, but carried herself so grown up. She seemed hard, and bitter, for some reason. That scared Beth. A young teenage boy walked up to her and put his arms around her. He gave her a tight squeeze. Karen reached up and stroked his head.

"Thank you Todd for being here," Karen said. She turned into his arms, and started sobbing. "It was such a tough time and she still lost the battle. Why do these bad things happen?"

"I know baby girl," said Todd. "Life is not fair. And what does it matter anyway?" Todd started stroking Karen's hair. She clutched him tighter, almost desperately. "When my Dad died of liver cancer," Todd continued. "I thought it was the end of the world, but then I realized, we all will die. We might as well feel good in the short time provided for us. Come with me. I have something that will ease that pain." Karen tucked tightly under Todd's arm as he lead her out to the parking lot.

"No," Beth groaned. The Professor changed the scene, and they were surrounded in cloud cover again. Beth's mom was weeping beside her. The Professor clutched both ladies close to him. Then Beth's mother disappeared.

"In the future, that will be your death, if you continue on your same self destructive path," said the Professor. "It can change, at least for a little while, but the last scene I am going to show you involves the cycle, or pattern, or whatever you want to call it. It is the ramifications of actions on others because of you." The clouds started to dissipate.

Beth watched as a run down old station wagon she had never seen before pulled to the curb in front of a house in a section of town she recognized. This was that neighborhood in Killeen, near Condor Park. It had been built around World War II. They currently lived in that neighborhood on Metropolitan Avenue.

Karen put the car in park and shut off the engine. She turned to the back seat and spoke to her three year old son.

"You stay right here Tripp," Karen said. "Mommy will be back in a little while."

"You said we were going to Mickey Dees," Tripp said.

"In a little while baby," Karen said. "I have got to get some stuff. If mommy doesn't get her stuff then mommy goes crazy. When mommy goes crazy, she takes a lot of people with her. Understand?"

Tripp nodded. He didn't really understand, but he knew not to argue with mommy when she said that. Karen pulled the car keys out of the ignition and exited the car leaving Trip inside by himself. She walked up to the door and rang the door bell.

"Well hello Karen," said a man in casual but expensive clothes as he answered the door. "What do I owe the honor of this visit?"

"I need a couple of grams of crack," said Karen. She could see over the man's shoulder into the living room where a large group of naked people, most of them male, were engaging in various acts of partying.

"I would need cash for that," said the man.

"Come on Benny," said Karen. "You know Todd is in jail. I don't have that kind of cash. I'll have to take it out in trade."

Benny opened the door a little bit wider and ushered Karen inside. "We are doing a shoot. A classy little number called *Gang Bang Girls Number 97*. We could use another girl. If you do your scenes as instructed, I will give you five grams plus a couple of C notes for the rest of life's worries."

"Thank you Benny," said Karen. She reached over and squeezed his arm. "You are a life saver." Karen entered the living room, which was also the movie set, and began to disrobe.

Three and a half hours later Karen returns to her car. She had taken a taste to get the edge off, but had restrained herself from going further because she was going to take Tripp to the McDonalds, and she so loved her Tripp. Karen glanced in the back and saw Tripp sleeping soundly on the back seat. She stumbled into the front seat, fished out her car keys, and started the car. Putting the car in drive, she took off down the street. About half a block down Metropolitan she side swiped a car with her passenger side.

"Whoops," Karen giggled. She was feeling pretty good. A man came out of a house and started yelling. "I'd better get out of here," Karen said. She floored the car and sped off down the road. When she got to Condor Street she swung a left, and headed towards Condor Park, W.S. Young Drive, and the McDonalds Restaurant. She stopped at the stop sign on Zepher. A KPD patrol car, lights flashing, was headed down Zepher. He slowed and looked at her and the damaged side of her car as he went by. The police car stopped.

Karen panicked and pushed the accelerator pedal to the floorboard. She got about fifty yards down the road before plowing into the back of a dark pick up truck. The hood of her car buckled. Antifreeze, oil, and gas leaked out into the road. Tripp, unsecured, was slammed into the back of the front seat. Karen, coming off her taste, was now scared and desperate. The Killeen Police Car now pulled in behind her, sirens a blaring. The police car stopped for several minutes.

Karen had one thing that Todd had given her, one thing for sure, and that was the old Ruger thirty-eight that was in her purse. Karen, discombobulated, grabbed her purse off the floor. Struggling she pulled the old revolver out of her purse.

"I love you Tripp," Karen said to an apparent empty back seat, and exited the station wagon while cocking the hammer of the gun. Tripp, hearing his name, started to regain consciousness, and began to move.

Officer Nix exited his cruiser, and drew his gun. "Ma'am," said Nix. "We don't have to do it this way. Please put the gun down." He continued to draw a bead on Karen who was about thirty feet away, which was too far away to have a fair chance at taking her gun away from her by physical ability before she could get a shot off.

Karen approached the cop. She heard Tripp groan in the back seat. Damn, she thought. She had promised the kid a happy meal, and by God she would get it for him. All she had to do was kill this cop.

Beth watched the scene unfold from three sides simultaneously, thanks to the Professor.

* * *

KPD Officer Nix screamed, "Lady, we don't have to do it this way, please!" By regulation he was supposed to shoot center of mass, but she was just a kid, and that would probably kill her. He diverted his aim to her right shoulder blade. He would not kill this one. She raised her gun and pointed it at his head. It was a double action gun; she cocked the hammer......

Officer Nix fired his weapon.

* * *

Karen just wanted to get to McDonalds. She finally had some money to spend on Tripp. The taste, she had taken at the house, was probably a little too strong, but now she just wanted it all to go away. Tripp was moaning, he probably had hurt himself. All she wanted was to get him to his Mickey Dees. He could have what ever he wanted. Karen loved Tripp. If she could make this cop go away then all would be alright. Todd had taught her how to cock and shoot the gun. She pulled the hammer back and pointed it at the monster.

A sharp pain in her neck made her whelp. She pulled the trigger, and fired her pistol. Then she collapsed on the ground. She saw flames all around herself.

* * *

Tripp heard his momma's voice and rose up from the floor boards where he had been violently thrown when the car had slammed into the back of the pick up truck. He tried to pull himself up. He managed to get one hand out the window and the other on the arm rest, and heave himself up when he heard a loud bang. His right hand, wrist snug against the rolled down window, disintegrated as the bullet slammed into it, and deflected toward his mom's neck and carotid artery. Tripp heard his mom yelp, and then heard another loud bang, and then flames were all around him. He was starting to burn.

* * *

"No, no, no, no no," screamed Beth! The Professor moved close to her, pulling her out of the scene. He wrapped his arms around her, and she collapsed weeping into his chest.

"It just takes a slight change in attitude, and the whole world will change," said the Professor. "Our impacts on the little ones are great. We need to take that seriously and with great responsibility."

Beth's weeping subsided, and she looked at the professor with fierce determination. "That scene we just saw," Beth said. "Will never, ever, ever, happen!" The Professor smiled down at her.

"You must change the attitude," said the Professor. "Forewarned of an event can prevent the event, but if the character does not change, it will just play itself out in another event. It is the outlook on life that is important. Break addictions. Enjoy life. Learn from the past, plan for the future, but live in the present. It really is as simple as that. Don't let things rule your life." The Professor paused, and scratched at his scruffy beard.

"The events you just saw will not happen now," continued the Professor. "Because I have shown them to you, but equally horrific events could happen if major changes don't happen in your life.

"You are forewarned," said the Professor. "And I think this will turn out good."

* * * * * * * *

Beth felt the car's movement and slammed on the brakes. The car in front of her continued, moving further and further away. The driver glanced back at Beth in his rear view mirror. The Army couple stared over at Beth's car, while the soldier moved in between them, and gently guided his family away from the stopped car. Beth collapsed against her steering wheel and began to weep.

"Mom," Karen said with real alarm in her voice. "Are you okay?" Karen, in a move that even shocked her, unbuckled her seat belt, and reached over for her mom. This only made Beth cry harder. Beth put the car in park, and hugged her daughter. They were both crying now. They stayed that way for several minutes.

"I'm okay baby, and I'm going to quit smoking," Beth said. Beth hugged Karen to her deeply. Beth and Karen sobbed into each other. After a few minutes the moment subsided.

"Its okay mamma," said Karen. "God's will be done. Todd told me that. His father is dying of liver cancer."

Beth recoiled in horror. "You must never see this Todd again." Beth said. She pushed Karen away.

"Mom," Karen cried. "He needs me. His dad is dying. Please mom, please!"

Beth remembered what the Professor had told her about forewarned could cause one horrific event to be replaced by another equal or even more horrific event. She had to be smart here. It was not a matter of trying to outsmart the system with specifics, but a matter of learning your lesson and doing the right thing. She was, by God, Karen's mom, and even though it would be hard, she had to teach principles to her daughter. She would not use the Professor's gift to her to try to outplay specific events. That was not its purpose. Beth actually felt stronger than she had in a long time.

"Of course baby," Beth said. "Todd needs you, and you are a wonderful person who helps others. I'm so sorry I snapped at you. We can overcome anything, because we face our problems head on. We are champions!"

Karen gave her mom a big hug. "I love you mom," Karen said. "We are champions!" Karen clutched her mom hard and began to cry again. Karen did not know why she was so emotional now, but something big was happening, and now she knew she was a champion who could handle it.

Beth put the car back in drive and moved away from the curb. "Let's go to work first," said Beth. "I need to talk to my boss. They are great people. They may be able to help me quit smoking. Then I will take the day off, and we will both spend time with Nanny. It will be a great day. And buckle that seat belt!"

"Yes ma'am," said Karen. She was giggling as she put her seat belt on. "It was totally delinquent of me ma'am. It won't happen again." Karen was feeling more relaxed than she had in a long time. She liked her mom's new slogan. We are champions was a lot better than; if mommy don't smoke, mommy goes crazy and takes a lot of people with her statement. Karen now had hope for a possible good future.

Beth wheeled the car into her second job at J&S Trucking. They were struggling. They didn't have the overtime to give her, but they paid her better than minimum wage, and they gave her bonuses when she made money for the company. They also took their losses without penalizing her, even when it was her fault. This was her favorite job. She truly wished this company well, and hoped for a future with it.

"Hi Bill," said Beth walking into his front office. Karen was in tow. Bill Beckerman, the Truck Manager, looked up in alarm.

"Well hi Beth. Hi Karen," said Bill, he looked very concerned. "Is everything okay? Why is Karen here?" Bill stood up. He was the nervous type. He had seen a lot of action in Vietnam, and people gave him his space. Later this would be diagnosed as PTSD, but this was 1984 and Bill was just considered high strung.

"Everything is fine Bill," said Beth. "I just need to talk to Jim or Susan. I'm going to quit smoking and I need their help."

"Sure," said Bill. "Jimbo is in back, working on a truck. Susan is collecting a bill. She should be back in ten minutes."

"I'll talk to Jim," said Beth. Bill stepped aside and let them pass. Bill scratched Karen's head as she walked by. Karen giggled, and gave him a couple of fake punches as she passed. Bill feigned injury, and gave them both a huge smile. Bill really loved these two.

"Hey Jim," said Beth, entering the garage. She was nervous as hell and physically shaking. "This is complete craziness," Beth continued. She was talking fast, trying to get it all out. "I met this quirky fellow in an alternate reality who called himself the Professor. He wants me to quit smoking, and to be a more positive role model for Karen. I know you think I'm nuts, but I need your help."

James Malone rolled out from under the truck he was working on. He gave Beth an odd smile. "You better sit down," he said. Karen sat in the folding chair next to the break table. Malone took the chair next to her, and put his hand on her hand.

"This would be a Professor Emit N. Relevart," stated Malone. Beth reeled and almost lost consciousness. This day was off the charts for weirdness.

"I would strongly recommend that you follow his advice," Malone continued while patting Beth's hand. Malone's wife Susan entered the shop. She was carrying a plastic tray containing three steaming beverages. She gave them both a big smile.

"French vanilla coffee with one cream," Susan said, and handed her husband a mug. "Your favorite drink, well, that is according to our mutual friend; the Professor." Jimbo Malone gave his wife a big smile as he accepted the mug.

"Beth," Susan said, as she handed Beth a mug. "Orange cinnamon tea with one sugar, for energy." Susan laughed, Beth giggled.

"How did you know?" Beth asked. She took the mug and took a sip. "It tastes divine."

"Well let's just say that our mutual friend recommended it," said Susan Malone. "And now, my favorite," she said, taking the remaining mug. She took the tray and threw it to the side. It instantly disappeared. Karen sat next to her mom in a folding chair at the break table. She looked around in fascinated wonder. Today was turning out to be a really great day.

* * *

The Professor looked out from his perch in an alternate reality. He took out his little black book, and turned to the page that had Beth and Karen's name on it. He wrote 'made it a couple of extra decades' by Beth's name. In parenthesis he wrote turned out to be a great mom and an excellent grandma. By Karen's name the Professor just wrote 'Matriarch.' He smiled as he envisioned all the future generations. Putting his book away he rubbed his face. His next assignment made him very nervous. He was going to visit his mortal self in the year 2011.

HOMECOMING

The Nevels were very proud. It had been a long eight months for Tom and Linda, but Joe was finally coming home. He was also coming home a hero, according to the letter they had received from the Department of the Army. Joe had earned several medals while fighting in Iraq. In their community of a little over a thousand people, only three had actually signed up for military service since the horrors of September eleventh.

Everybody had talked about it. I mean hell, it was the number one topic of conversation, but only three had signed up. Of those three only Joe had volunteered for Infantry duty in the United States Army. The Nevels had a lot to be proud of, and now Joe was coming home.

They had got the letter in today's mail. Joe was supposed to call when he got to San Francisco on the eighth, and that was tomorrow. He should be home two days after that. That gave them just three days to plan, organize, and put together Joe's homecoming celebration. It would be a grand affair with a parade and a big banquet. The whole town would be involved. Linda immediately started making phone calls. Tom went to see the Mayor to arrange the use of the town hall.

Linda had just finished reading Betty, her neighbor, the typed letter she had received from Joe, when the call waiting tone beeped in. Checking the caller ID she noticed an unfamiliar area code. Thinking it could be from Joe, she signed off with Betty and took the call.

"Hello," Linda said. She was suddenly nervous.

"Mom," Joe's voice resounded through the receiver. Tears came to Linda's eyes.

"Joe," she said. "It is so great to hear from you. We love you so much. We have missed you so much. We are so proud of you. You must have gotten home early. When are you coming home?"

"Tomorrow," Joe said. His voice had a sad and tired tone to it.

"Oh Joe," Linda beamed. "That will be great. We have to work fast here now. Nancy, your old girlfriend will be glad to see you. She has been seeing that good for nothing Alex, but when my war hero son comes home, and the whole town turns out for the celebration, well, she'll come running back to you. We are having this big celebration, with parades and speeches. We will have to move it up because you're coming home early and…"

"Mom," Joe interrupted. "I don't want a celebration. I need to ask you something."

"No celebration," Linda quipped. "That's nonsense. There will be a parade, and you marching as the guest of honor. There will be…."

"Mom," Joe interrupted again. "I must ask you something."

"Okay son," said Linda. "Ask your question, and then we can get back to planning your celebration, and knock off all this other silliness."

Joe took a deep breath, let out a sigh, and began, "I have a buddy, an Army friend who I want to bring home with me. He has nowhere else to go."

"Well sure son," Linda said. "We can put him up at the hotel."

"Mom," Joe jumped in. "He can't stay at the hotel. He was pretty badly injured in the war. He needs someone to take care of him."

At that moment Tom came home. Linda motioned him over to her.

"Hold on Joe," she said. "Your Dad is here." To Tom she whispered, "Pick up the other phone, it's Joe. He wants to bring home a wounded war buddy."

Tom picked up the other line and said, "Joe, it's so great to talk to you. We are so very proud of you. We have got big plans for when you get home. Now what is this your Mom is saying about a wounded war buddy?"

Joe began again, "Mom, Dad. He has nowhere else to go. His Bradley was hit by a missile. He lost both his legs, he is horrible burned on his face and upper body, and he is blind."

There was a long moment of silence. Linda was staring at Tom with a look of deep concern. Finally Tom said, "Joe, this is quite the burden. This fellow would need constant care. How long do you plan on keeping him?"

There was another silence, shorter this time, and then Joe said, "Well Dad, he has nowhere else to go. He would stay with us indefinitely." Linda let out a gasp.

"Joe," Tom said. "I understand you wanting to take care of your war buddy. It is very commendable, but you do realize what a horrible burden this would be?" Doesn't the Army have facilities to take care of people like this? I mean, I feel for his loss, and yours too son, but you've got a life. This shouldn't have to be our problem."

Linda chimed in with, "We don't mean to be cruel, but that would totally rearrange all our lives. Especially, yours, son."

There was another short silence, and then Joe said, "I understand, but I had to ask."

Tom jumped in, "Please don't be mad at us son."

"No," Joe said. "In fact I'm actually a little relieved. That is a big weight off my shoulders. I'll see you tomorrow, I love you."

"We love you too, and are so proud of you," Linda and Tom said together.

When the line went dead, Linda looked at Tom with deep concern etched on her face.

"It's okay," said Tom. "War changes people, but he will be okay. It is best this way." Tom and Linda hugged. It was a deep desperate hug. It was the first time they hugged like that since September eleventh.

The strangeness of the phone call was forgotten as Tom and Linda leaped into their chores of preparing for the homecoming celebration. It was past midnight when they fell exhausted into bed, but they somehow managed to muster the energy to make love. That was something else they hadn't done in a long time, since before September eleventh.

Tom and Linda were awakened at nine o'clock the next morning by the doorbell. Every thirty seconds thereafter came a firm three raps knocked. The knock had an authoritarian and infinitely patient air to it. It was very spooky. Within a couple of minutes Tom and Linda had roused themselves, grabbed robes and rushed downstairs.

What greeted them was not their son, but an Army officer decked out in full dress uniform. They let him in, and he ushered them to take a seat in their own living room. They complied without hesitation. The Army Officer remained standing.

Ma'am, Sir," the officer began. "My name is Captain Tousinski, United States Army. On Behalf of the President of the United States, and the Secretary of The Army, "it is with the deepest condolence that we inform you of the death of your son, Specialist-four Joseph P. Nevel."

At this point Linda gasped and clutched her chest. Tom stiffened and his eyes became moist. The Captain continued without interruption, "Recipient of the Silver Star, the Purple Heart, Army Commendation Medal, and the Combat Infantryman's Badge. His loss will be greatly felt by this nation."

There was a long pause. Finally Tom meekly asked, "But how? We just talked to him yesterday."

The Captain softened his stance and expression a bit. He almost looked human for a moment. "It was yesterday afternoon, sir, it was a suicide.

His body will be flown in tonight. I am the notification officer, a causality assistance officer......"

Captain Tousinski paused and pulled out a business card, and handed it to Tom. Then he continued, "A Captain Tim Ryan will arrive with the body. He will assist you in any way possible. He will have the answers to your questions."

Sometime during the long silence, Captain Tousinski turned and walked away. Tom and Linda did not register hearing the door close. They sat in shocked silence.

They were not any better composed as they waited for the C130 airplane, carrying Joe's body, to taxi to a halt, and open its back ramp. Linda rocked back and forth clutching an imaginary infant Joe while muttering, "My baby," over and over again.

Tom spent all his effort fighting back tears. A young officer in Dress Greens departed the plane and approached them.

"Ma'am, Sir," he said while glancing at each of them in turn. "My name is Captain Ryan, on behalf of the..."

"Enough Captain," Tom cut him off. "We'd like to see the body. We just talked to our son yesterday. He seemed fine then. Maybe the Army has made some kind of horrible mistake."

Captain Ryan considered for a moment, shrugged, and said, "Yes sir, please follow me sir."

They approached a coffin draped in an American flag. Captain Ryan removed the flag, opened the coffin, and stepped aside.

Although the face was badly burned, they could easily recognize their son, Joe. Tom was the first to understand the gravity of what had happened. Being a war veteran himself he accepted it, and dealt with it with a steady stream of silent tears originating from his aching soul. Linda was a little slower on the uptake. When realization finally dawned on her she handled it with hysterical wailing, and threw herself on the coffin that contains their son Joe. Joe's corpse was legless, horrible burned on his face and upper body, and missing both his eyes.

Edwards Brothers Malloy
Thorofare, NJ USA
May 23, 2016